GREENER ON THE OTHER SIDE

Written by Lionel Ntasano

Published by New Generation Publishing in 2014

Copyright © Lionel Ntasano 2014

First Edition

The author asserts the moral right under the Copyright, Designs and Patents Act 1988 to be identified as the author of this work.

All Rights reserved. No part of this publication may be reproduced, stored in a retrieval system or transmitted, in any form or by any means without the prior consent of the author, nor be otherwise circulated in any form of binding or cover other than that which it is published and without a similar condition being imposed on the subsequent purchaser.

www.newgeneration-publishing.com

New Generation Publishing

To my parents Oscar and Prisca

You have done right by me. I dedicate this book to you in honor of your sacrifice, wisdom and perseverance.

"The world is a tragedy to those who feel, but a comedy to those who think."

– HORACE WALPOLE

Preface

I remember one particular day, after fiercely arguing with my girlfriend at the time, I decided to get some air at the beach in Bujumbura city – My city! As I started walking on the sand, my headphones on, listening to some Sade and trying to calm down and control my emotions, I saw a group of people gathered.

I instantly felt chaos in the atmosphere. I heard screams and people arguing. I got attracted by the sudden commotion and low mumbles. I found my way into the crowd, and to my utter surprise, I saw a half-naked woman holding a large beer bottle. She was drunk out of her mind and fervently venting her frustration to the crowd about how she had lost her husband to a fishing trip with his two usual fishing partners. She lamented how one fateful day the three of them went on a fishing trip together as they always did. At the end of that day, only two of them came back. Her husband was missing. At that particular time, there was a shortage of fish, fishermen weren't reaching their normal quotas. Anxiety was rampant, as their catch was their livelihood, and she accused them of having thrown her husband into the lake. She explained to the crowd how they did so as a form of sacrifice to whatever creature or mermaid-God that ruled the deep waters in order to appease it so that it could release the flow of fish. It sounded absurd, and I could not believe what I was hearing. She further explained how she had never been the same since. She searched for any information that could lead to her missing husband and she went to the police but to no avail. She went to see pastors, gurus and witch-doctors, to get justice I presume. Nothing worked. Frustrated, she started eating disorderly and drinking alcohol to alleviate her distress. The trauma destroyed her and annihilated her energy, rendering her hopeless and confused to the point of hallucination.

Having heard enough, I walked away and sat under a palm tree to ponder on the story. I started thinking about the argument with my girlfriend, and then of my older brother whom I hadn't seen for many years - it made think and ponder about *happiness*. I wondered what made it so fleeting, and I realized that I actually did not know what it meant. Was it love? Was it the ability to love? Was it the sensation of being loved unconditionally? Could it be security? Peace? What about the stillness of the mind?

As I pondered some more, I got stuck on the idea of *hope*. Could hope be the precursor of happiness? *Why does the grass always seem to be greener on the other side of the fence?* I asked myself. I reasoned that everybody is in love with and irrationally attached to the concept of what could be. That is the essence and wealth of a youthful mind: having options and having the ability to dream. Reality is probably just too boring, slow and unengaging. That little fantasy of ours, that little secret, is the only thing that keeps us going. Some people call it hope, while others view it as goals. Spiritual souls call it faith, while the professionals call it vision. I found it odd how happiness lay always in the future, never in the present. It intrigued me why we humans perceive the grass to always be greener on the other side of the fence. What are the factors or behaviors that make us so unhappy, always needing and wanting things or situations that ultimately make us so unhappy?

I decided to write some of these ideas in my tiny

diary, so that I could later send an email discussing them with my best friend Aristide. However, when I finished writing the email, I saved it rather than sending it. When I later re-read the unsent email, I noticed that it formed the basis of a book, but never thought too much about it and went on with my usual business.

In a serendipitous, eye-opening moment, I experienced another intriguing evening a few months later with a group of friends. While enjoying some coffee, we started bragging about how much fun we had had the previous night at a popular night club, boasting about how much money we had spent on champagne and liquor. We quickly realized how frivolous we had become with our newly acquired wealth, weather earned or inherited, and; we decided to use our funds in a more productive and respectful way. We therefore decided to feed some of the plentiful street kids that forever roam our city.

To this day, I am not exactly sure if our intentions were quite right. Were we really trying to really make a difference, or was it just to alleviate our guilt? However, what I am sure of is that the more vocal leaders in the group used some moral duress to induce everybody to participate.

A few weeks later, after planning and organizing sessions interrupted by arguments, tantrums and social-positioning tactics fueled by hidden agendas, we were finally ready for the big day. The night before, proud at the progress of our endeavor, we found ourselves drinking, partying and spending more money than any other previous night spent together. We outdid ourselves, and actually stayed up until dawn. We got into bar fights and drove around town like mad men, laughing like the world owed us everything. When we arrived at the site, some of the participants had disappeared - a few had gone home, others had switched off their phones, and those left had no energy left to be productive. The missing individuals started reappearing one by one, hours late and looking like zombies: tired, sluggish and scared of approaching the kids. We got into petty arguments, insulting each other and blaming each other in front of the kids. Yet somehow, we managed to pull ourselves together. We cooked, served and played with the kids, and when all the kids had been served and started eating, we were all standing together watching them in awe and amazement at what we had managed to do. We were all quiet and content to see the faces of the kids, eating and having fun. At that moment I felt proud of myself and was amazed at what teamwork could achieve.

However, I witnessed on that day that I will never understand: when the food came, all the kids rushed and fought to get the pieces of meat that were scattered and hidden in the rice and beans. They pushed and shoved each other to get them, and once they found them, they stowed as many as they could in palms or pockets, then started eating the rest, saving the meat for last or later. One little girl struggled to eat with one hand as she had a handful of meat in the other, and some of the rice fell in her juice, ruining it. Another little girl sitting next to her noticed what had happened and started laughing at her and began taunting and teasing her just because she did not have as many pieces of meat as the others. The struggling girl took some of the rice and put it in the cup of the girl who was laughing at her and started laughing as well, making the first laughing girl cry.

I was dumbfounded by these acts. That night before going to sleep, I mentally replayed all these eye-opening events: the two fishermen, the mad woman, my friends, the partying, the alcohol, the hidden agendas, the reckless spending, the arguments, the kids, everything. I began asking myself questions that prompted me to finally write this book.

What makes us do what we do?
What makes you do what you do?

We all live busy lives, and sometimes we fail to take the time to truly reflect on what we do and why we do it. Have you really thought and asked yourself in a self reflective way why you do what you do? When you think about it now, does it make sense? Does it make you happy? Does it serve a specific purpose? Does it serve an idea? Does it serve a palpable objective? Will it preserve or honor your livelihood? Does it really? Do you think before you act or is it just a feeling, an emotion that takes over your body, numbing the side of your brain that creates rational thinking. Ninety-nine percent of all our mistakes in life are based on actions rooted in emotion.

What is this feeling, this emotion? Obviously it is the root of everything that has happened to us, is happening to us now, and will happen to us in the future. I am afraid to say this, but this sensation or feeling is who you and I really are. It will definitely determine everything that happens to you and me during the course of our life span.

So why don't we do everything in our mental, physical and spiritual power to learn about this feeling - learn how to contain it, learn how to control it. As a race, we are capable of extraordinary feats. If you take a few minutes to look, understand and reflect on how the human race has evolved, you would be greatly impressed, but you would also be confused as to how we have been unable to master this feeling.

According to scientists, our earliest human ancestors

ventured onto grasslands of Africa about six million years ago. These early humans were exceptionally weak and vulnerable creatures, but they managed to transform themselves into the most astounding hunters on the planet within a short period of time compared to any other species within evolution's time scale. Based on one of my favorite author's book *Robert Greene's Mastery*, they managed to do so thanks to two key biological traits: the *visual* and the *social*.

You see, animals are locked in a perpetual present. Most mammals' visual systems are built for scanning, with a limited ability to learn from the past events. This is due to the fact that they are easily distracted by what is in front of their eyes. However, our ancestors overcame this basic animal weakness by developing a visual system built for depth of focus. This meant that by looking long enough at any object and managing not to get distracted even for a very short period, they could temporarily withdraw themselves from their immediate surroundings. This in turn heightened their analytical skills, enabling them to notice patterns, make generalizations, and think ahead. In their struggle to find food and fend off and avoid predators, this emerging ability to withdraw and think quickly became their primary advantage. It connected them to a reality that other animals could not access.

The second, subtler, biological advantage is the social, which is even more powerful. Early humans depended on social cohesion, and they did so in order to create as they explored open areas. This social intelligence became increasingly sophisticated, which allowed these early humans to cooperate with one another at a very high level. This intelligence depended on deep attention and focus, as an understanding of the natural environment was imperative. Misreading the social signs in a tight-knit group could prove highly dangerous, so they developed complex social groupings. To adapt to this, they evolved mirror neurons. This meant that they could not only imitate those around them, but also imagine what others might be thinking and feeling, heightening the degree of cooperation.

With the invention of language and the reasoning powers it brought them, our ancestors could take this insightful ability further: seeing pattern in people's behavior and deducing their motivations. Over the years, these reasoning skills have become infinitely more powerful and refined, making human kind king of the food chain - in other words, rulers of their surroundings. However, these highly developed reasoning powers and close social cohesion brought in a new aspect to our livelihood that is only possessed by humans: *morality*. This is when it all went downhill.

In order to create this sense of cohesion, these early humans established all kinds of codes of behavior, taboos, and shared rituals. They also created myths in which their tribe was considered to be the favorite of the Gods, chosen for some great purpose. To be a member of the tribe was to be cleansed by rituals and to be favored by the Gods, and those who belonged to other groups, with unfamiliar rituals and belief systems, were not clean. They represented the other: something dark, threatening, and a challenge to the tribe's sense of superiority. It transformed itself into a great fear of other cultures and ways of thinking. It has presently reached a form of mental process in which we divide the world into what is familiar and unfamiliar, clean and unclean.

German philosopher Immanuel Kant viewed the ability of human beings to reason as the basis of our status as the premier moral agents. He argued that morality is grounded in reason not in tradition, intuition, conscience, emotion or attitudes such as sympathy. To be fully human is to be a rational being capable of exercising both reason and free will in making and choosing actions. Others believe that morality is grounded in spirituality in the sense that a desire for a higher moral life is based on fear and a promise of a heavenly life in the future. However, the bottom line is that most activity in life is based on a moral or immoral consideration of *motives*.

I truly believe it is the motive that makes the virtue a means to achieve a given end. And this given end is *pleasure*. But the truth is that no aspect of our mental life is more important to the quality and meaning of our existence than *emotions*. They are what makes life is worth living. No matter who you are, or what you have achieved, everybody always looks ahead, imagining themselves on their death bed trying to wonder what their last thoughts would be. I can assure you that it would be the moments and people that gave them the most pleasure. These emotions can be summed up in seven vices and their seven corresponding virtues.

They go as follows: pride vs humility, envy vs kindness, gluttony vs abstinence, lust vs chastity, wrath vs patience, greed vs liberality and sloth vs diligence. Try and remember or imagine any emotion that you have ever felt in your life, and I promise you that it is one hundred percent rooted in at least one of these vices or virtues. You might be wondering why I call it *a feeling* when there are seven of them. My views on these feelings are that people probably have all seven vices in their hearts and minds, as they are humans, but there is always one vice that is more pertinent in each one of us - one that is almost impossible to change unless you use deep rational thought by asking yourself why. It is one that is more ingrained in our souls, and one that we are unaware of. A good example would be to tell someone his vice and watch his reaction. Usually he would get defensive, argumentative and angry due to the fact that he believes it not to be true. Truth be told, he reacts this way because he cannot recognize himself as the person you tell he is. Most people see themselves as kinder, more genuine, but mainly as doing the right thing according to their situation. Fortunately, each one of these seven vices has an opposite corresponding holy virtue that lies dormant in all our hearts.

Nevertheless, I truly believe that these holy virtues are only triggered by the mind, as our mental capacity is the only element that separates us from animals, because I can assure you that these vices will take everyone to their doom. Each one of them has a thousand different ways of destroying a person:

>-*Lust* and its excessive desires and love shown in uncontrolled passions and pleasure-seeking activities, often leading to sexual indecency and perversions. Triggered by what women and men see with their eyes.

>-*Gluttony* and its over-indulgence and over-consumption of anything to the point of waste.

>-*Greed* and its excessive need for the accumulation of wealth, especially for personal gain, triggering disloyalty, deliberate betrayal, treason, bribery, scavenging, trickery or manipulation of authority and hoarding of materials or objects.

>-*Sloth* and its apathy, discontent, joylessness, melancholy, depression, sadness and despair with one's current situation.

-*Wrath* and its uncontrolled feelings of hatred and anger.

-*Envy* and its desire to compare oneself to others in terms of money, looks, coolness, intelligence, popularity, or any number of categories.

-*Pride* is considered the original and most serious of the seven vices, and the ultimate source from which the others arise. It is the excessive love of self with a consuming desire to be more important than others.

The journey and stories you are about to embark on in this book are of ordinary people just like you and me who kill themselves everyday in order to feel alive.

Lionel M. Ntasano, October 30th 2012

NICKOLAS JORDAN

- THE PRIEST -

CHAPTER ONE

It was pitch black and very quiet, with the stench of cigarette smoke clogging up the room. He was laying there, eyes wide open, almost lifeless on his queen bed - one pillow on the floor, the other cupped in his arm pit. It was maddeningly soundless, but he suddenly heard thunder breaking up the silence. It is hot, humid and musty outside, he thought to himself. Airplane, he concluded as he got up to get some water to quench his raging thirst. His skin was sticky with sweat as he tiptoed through the small kitchen to the fridge. As he opened the fridge door, he heard unusual meowing, as if a distressed baby was crying. "What the hell" he whispered in confusion and fear. A cat he thought to himself as he proceeded to open the water bottle.

He was drowsy and did not bother to fetch a glass, so he gulped the cold water down his throat, breathing heavily as if he had finished running a marathon. "Help me Ô Lord" he whispered to himself.

He paused in thought, standing motionless as a statue. Nicholas was bothered, but could not find the source of his anxiety. It was 2am and he could not find any sleep. Was it Belinda's recent abortion? Was it the fact that Levy was getting married, or that Stan was not answering his phone calls? Was it the fact that some neighborhood teenagers had started calling him *Black Jesus* for the past few weeks and did not act upon it? Or was it the fact that attendance at Mass was poor earlier in the day? So many thoughts raced through his mind without him rationally examining each one of them accordingly.

This was not typical of Father Nickolas, who usually had the temperance of a saint. He was patient, logical, acutely observant and earnestly listened to any one he encountered. Even before he was ordained as a priest, he had a refreshing knack of making people around him feel like someone was really listening to them. Early on in his life, he quickly understood that ego has the biggest place in people's souls. Some are bigger than others, some very small, but ego is always at the center.

Father Nick, as he was better known, was a young priest. He was thirty-nine years old, but looked twenty-nine, and tall (well over six feet), with neatly defined facial features. His clean goatee was thin enough to see his deep dimples, and his teeth were straight and clearly whitened, with a small but charming gap between the two front teeth. His lips were almost purple in color due to his heavy smoking. He had clear white eyes with a powerful piercing look that almost never blinked, yet was tremendously welcoming and insinuated trustfulness and intelligence. He was graced with fair, even chocolate skin, enhanced by his lean muscle tone. He had an athletic build with bowed legs as he played varsity tennis in college. He kept his hair natural, but well groomed, with a string of intruding white hair on the right side of his head.

- He kept telling people jokingly that back in Africa where he came from, having white hair at a very young age was a sign of future financial wealth. He never took the time to mention exactly where in Africa he came from, because the people he met in New York City never knew much about the continent, let alone the names of the different countries within the respective continent. He only mentioned *Burundi* when pressed for details.

Father Nick was born in 1974 in Gitega, the second biggest city of Burundi, the oldest of four boys. His father was an agricultural agent for the country's main State-owned agriculture and environment company. His mother manned the small shop they owned in the city center, which sold basic necessities: everything from candles to condoms. He was born in an era when the State was the predominant employer and private investment was discouraged. Bars were closed during working hours, and the people spent a lot of time on betrothal ceremonies like weddings and funerals. They lived a modest living, but the family managed their earnings well and never lacked basic necessities. His parents practised quietness and order, and instilled self-control in their children. They always reminded them to keep their thoughts to themselves, to face tragedy stoically and to be very polite. That was the Burundian notion of proper behavior.

On the fateful night of 20 October 1993, when he was just about to turn nineteen years old, the country entered in what would become one of Africa's longest civil wars. Some factions in the army attacked the Presidential Palace in the capital city, killing the President, the Speaker and the Deputy Speaker of the National Assembly. For five days there was no government. As the news of the President's death spread, violence erupted all over the country. Tutsis (Nicholas' ethnic tribe found in the Great Lakes region) were targeted and killed, and roads were blocked to delay the army's inevitable response. Some claimed that this response was planned, like the 1994 genocide in neighboring Rwanda, which shares the same ethnic tribes. There was no evidence that this was on a national level, but the speed of the mobilization suggested that some people had feared this could happen and made preparations. It was estimated that during those first days, over 50,000 Tutsis were killed.

The country's historical cohesive social structure was classified as Tutsis, Hutus and Twas. The Hutus were the majority, the Tutsis the minority, while the Twas only represented 1% of the population. The Tutsis and Hutus spoke the same language, had the same culture, worshiped the same God and honored the same king. It was a stable, almost feudal, system, but it was not idyllic or harmonious. Just as peasants were exploited in Europe in the Middle Ages, there was a degree of repression by the Hutus. Revolts by Hutu peasants were not unknown and the King's army was composed mainly of Tutsis.

Radical Hutus during this 1993 crisis liked to emphasize these deep historical roots of conflict, including the 1972 tragedy incurred at their expense, where 3,000 Tutsis and 200,000 Hutus lost their lives. All in all, things were about to get worse.

Before the crisis began, young Nicholas was still in high school and had found a small job at a coffee bean assembly plant co-owned by Michel and Sigourney Pécresse. They were a French and American couple who owned a coffee company in the USA that worked with the government, and had fallen in love with the country, the people and especially the coffee. Nicholas befriended Michel when he subtly pointed out to him the pilfering that was going on behind his back. Michel was intrigued by the boy's wisdom, and they developed a mentor-student relationship. Nicholas was attracted by the mogul's brutal honesty, passion and energy. They both had a fanatical love for basketball and the Chicago Bulls. Nicholas and his younger brothers were attending school (*école normale*) in Kibimba set up by the Friends Evangelical Church (Quakers).

Early on the horrendous morning of 21st October, Nicholas had spent the night at the Pécresses' house because he had worked late the night before and usually spent the night there, when he did. He was still wearing the company uniform as he rushed out of the compound to make it to class on time. It was too early for him to listen to the radio. On the road he met some small groups of people who he thought were just going to the market, but he soon saw that things were not normal: there were armed people making barriers.

He saw teachers returning home instead of continuing to work. He was exhausted and untidy. Without thinking too much about it, he decided to head home as well. On his way to his house, he noticed that he did not have his keys, so he took a small detour back to the Pécresses' house. When he reached the gate, he bent over to pick a tiny stone to knock with. He knew that Nepo the gardener was slightly deaf and scatter-brained. As he knocked, he could hear Poutchi the German shepherd barking furiously, letting everyone know that someone was at the gate. Nepo came hurrying, barefoot and with no shirt, his beer belly bouncing all over the place. He opened the peep hole first to see who was at the gate. He recognized Nick. "Young man, why are you back?" Nepo asked, getting irritated. "They are not here" he quickly followed. "Nepo stop joking, I forgot my keys. Let me in," Nick replied.

Nepo saw the seriousness on the boy's face and let him in without saying a word. Poutchi recognized Nick and jumped up, trying to lick his face. Nick ignored it and walked straight to the backyard to the dormitories.

As he entered the common room where he had spent the night, he searched for his keys under all the mattresses and found them. On his way out, he heard someone screaming in French and people running. He recognized Michel's voice and quickly ran to the front of the house, where he saw Claude the driver starting the engine of the land cruiser and Michel giving orders to some other workers. He noticed that Michel was agitated, with his Berretta tucked in his waistband. There was definitely something wrong. One of the workers looked at Nick, which made Michel look back. Nick saw despair in Michel's eyes as he said "you are coming with me, I will explain in the car". Nick just stood there and nodded, understanding that there was no need for extra words.

Michel summoned two of his security guards, who carried handguns and looked like they meant business. They were former soldiers, and preferred working as private security agents because the pay and living conditions were more promising. Nickolas entered the vehicle through the fifth small door in the rear. "He doesn't need to come along," one of the guards whispered to Michel, who for the first time sat in the passenger seat next to Claude. "I need him!" Michel shouted back, stunning the soldier with his authority.

The plant was about 147 acres long. They needed to get on the other side of the plant to the administrative blocks quickly because the buildings were being burned down. Michel had received the news over his walkie-talkie that a riot had broken down by the lower Hutu workers. The reason for their mutiny was that Hutus never got the better-paying office jobs that were always given to the Tutsies.

Claude's driving was frantic, ignoring the potholes and trying to reach to his destination as fast as he could, making his anxious passengers car-sick in the process. He slowed down abruptly in front of a chaotic scene almost made for an epic Hollywood movie. "Oh my

God," Michel exclaimed in a high-pitched voice as he opened his door while the car still moving.

The guards followed suit. "We are going to kill all of them!" shouted one of the arsonists, challenging Michel. The arsonist's eyes were popping out with the adrenaline and mixed emotions, hatred and vindication showing on his face with a devilish smirk. "They took everything from us, now it's our turn to take what is rightfully ours," the lead arsonist exclaimed.

The angry hooded and cagouled men, surrounded the lead arsonist, screamed and squalled in elixir at the end of every sentence the lead arsonist spoke. "It's time to cut the tall trees" the Hutu incendiary added referring to the taller looking Tutsis. Even bigger cheers came from of the hooded men, who brandished batons, machetes and menacing sticks. There were about forty of them, dancing and running around like mad men burning up their asylum.

Right at that moment Michel felt alone and out of place. There was no one to call on to protect him - no authorities, no uncorrupt police. Even with his gun and security officers, this was not his fight. However, he was more concerned and disturbed by what he was hearing and witnessing. *Decadence* was the first word that came to his mind. "Sigourney" he said under his breath.

He started slowly walking back to the car. He knew that his time in Burundi was over, and understood that it was imperative for him to leave as soon as he could. As Michel came back to the car, distraught, he caught Nick's eyes. The boy had stayed in the car the whole time, fearing for his life. He was almost in tears, as he had witnessed everything. Michel told him that he had to find his family and stay safe the best way he could.

They hurried back to the main house to drop Michel off. He gave orders to the driver and security to drop

Nick at his home, and they did exactly what was asked of them except that when they reached at the boy's home, there was nobody there. In fact, the entire Tutsi neighborhood was empty. "Come back in" Claude the driver ordered Nick. "You will wait with us at the old man's house," he added, referring to Michel, while starting the engine. And so they headed back to the Pécresses' house to seek refuge while they planned their next move.

CHAPTER TWO

At round 12am, Nick got woken up by the commotion of yet another fracas at the front of the house, cutting short his dream about his family. He could hear people crying. It felt as if the sky had fallen in. Nick rushed to the front of the house, where he found a group of people surrounding what looked like a heavily wounded man. He was shirtless and barefooted. He was bleeding profusely.

It was drizzling, but nobody cared or seemed to notice, as the news they had just received had turned their lives upside down. Some women even fainted. Sigourney was tending the poor guy with her first aid kit, but could not do much. As Nick approached the crowd, he saw Michel inside the house on the phone talking frantically and throwing his hands in the air as if the person on the other end of the line could see his frustration. He also noticed packed bags and a few suitcases. As he reached the crowd, they lifted the wounded man and put him in the back of one of the land cruisers headed for the nearest operational clinic. Nick heckled one flimsy guy from the crowd and questioned him on the wounded man. "What happened?" Nick asked.

The man explained that he was a teacher who had escaped an execution. "What are you talking about?" Nick howled. "He was blocked from going to work in the morning. He is a teacher at école normale. So he returned home." As the man was about to continue explaining, Michel approached them and stood by Nick. The conversation changed into French in order for Michel to understand. "My brothers and I go to school there," Nick said. "Well, a few hours after returning home, people came and tied him and his neighbors up and carried them off to the petrol station on the main road." The man carried on with his story, swallowing his own spit and taking a deep breath as he continued to explain what had happened.

They were held outside all day. At around 4pm rain began to fall and they took them inside the petrol station. It looked serious, as if they had a list of the names of Tutsis. There were students, other teachers, neighbors and accountants, but they all had one thing in common: their ethnicity. They kept bringing more people until there was no room for any more – not only officials but also peasants. In the evening they started drinking beer that they had taken from nearby stores after the traders had fled. They had started to get drunk. They threw stones at the hostages. Those with spears and machetes started jabbing at them. One man brought some petrol and told the others to set it alight and burn them alive. When they had finished counting heads, they wanted to do their worst, which, was to hit them on the head and make them unconscious or stab them to death. Some of the victims were too tired to stand up and had to lie down. They had brought a corrugated roofing sheet, which they used to pour petrol down into the crowd, and they burned tires. At around 10pm the wounded man was able to escape from the filling station through God's power. "God? Where is God today? How can you believe in God or a God on a day like this one?" Nick asked. "There was some window," the man continued, ignoring Nick's comment. "They found some old sacks, as the place had been used in the past for selling coffee. Your coffee, sir." Michel remained silent.

They used these sacks to protect themselves from

being overpowered by the smoke. Together with another guy called François, who later died, they used a table to reach and break a window. He wanted to die as soon as possible, but not to be burned alive. He grabbed the top of the window with both hands and jumped. He began to run. He got followed, so he slid down on his stomach into a ditch just as heavy rain started pouring down. He remained there for about an hour, listening to the heavy rain falling on the petrol station roof and the ghastly noise of the slaughter. There was too much noise. It was hard for him to concentrate, for he was starving and thirsty.

He passed through the forest, reaching his school and finding nobody there. He wanted to reach the Ndava commune where his brother-in-law lived, but luckily he recognized Claude, your driver his friend on one of his errands. This was how he found himself here.

Nick could not make sense of what was happening. Things were moving too fast. He had no idea where his family was, and he was dirty, distraught, alone and confused. He approached the jeep hoping to get more information before the man was taken to the clinic. Michel felt helpless watching Nick walk almost aimlessly towards the jeep. "I am a student at the same school you teach. Do you recognize me or my brothers?" Nick asked the surviving infirm. "I know you. You are Jerome Bucumi's son. Dear God! Son, you should find any relatives that you have and leave this God forsaken country before it is too late," the man replied, choking on his own spit. "Why do you say that?" Nick asked, bowing his head to weep. "Your brothers and parents where there. They were there from the beginning, son." the man added.

Nick turned around, looking at Michel and Sigourney. His heart was pounding hard and fast. His breathing quickened as he started sweating and his face scrunched up in deep sorrow. He could not breathe, and tears poured profusely. He screamed in agony and cried his heart out, falling on his knees screaming, *"Why God, why God why?"* The couple tended to him immediately, holding him tight. There was nothing they could do at that moment to soothe his pain or predicament.

Seventy Tutsi schoolgirls, boys, teachers and working men and women were burned to death on that night in a petrol station, including Nick's family. The events of October 1993 in Burundi have been regarded as the most successful failed coup in history, and were condemned internationally. The country was in chaos. Burundi did not need another stroke of bad luck, but this was to come in April 1994 when a notorious plane crash killed the interim President and neighboring Rwandese President and launched the heavily publicized Rwandan genocide. The country entered into a civil war, and foreigners were evacuated.

Michel and Sigourney left four days after the killings at the filling station. They left everything they owned but took Nickolas with them to the USA as a political refugee through their deep connections. They provided for him and helped him settle into, in his new life. It wasn't new or uncomfortable for them, as they had adopted two other children before: an orphan girl from Korea and a boy from Vietnam. Nickolas learned English quickly and went to college, graduating with honors in psychology. He got an American citizenship after seven years, taking his name from his idol Michael Jordan, and under the name of Nickolas Jordan wrote a book called *Cleaning up the Ghetto -Tales of the Minority* about his own life and what happened in his home country on that night.

The bestselling published book earned him more book deals and a full scholarship to Harvard University, where he earned a Masters degree in theology focusing on biblical research. He was only twenty-eight years old. Two years later he was ordained as a priest in the Roman Catholic Church.

The events of October 1993 forever shaped Nick's view on life and influenced every decision that he took. It shaped his values, as he had witnessed the worst of mankind while paradoxically witnessing the greatest compassion. On the plane journey to USA, he concluded that most of life is hell, filled with failure and loss. People disappoint you, dreams don't work out, hearts get broken and innocent people die. The best moments of life when everything came together were very few and fleeting, but he could never get to the next great moment if he didn't keep going, and that is what he did: he kept going. He decided to be a beacon of light to whoever needed guidance.

Before the burning, Nicholas was a naïve, sensitive and vulnerable boy. He entered this world remarkably weak and helpless, and for this he received great sheltering and comfort from his parents. In turn he idealized his parents. His survival depended on their strength and reliability. He came to view their actions through the lens of his needs, and in turn they became an extension of him. Inevitably he saw them as stronger, more capable and more selfless than they really were. He often transferred these idealizations and distortions to teachers, and friends, projecting on to them what he wanted and needed to see. His view of people became saturated with various emotions: worship, admiration, love, need and anger. Then in his adolescence he started to glimpse a less than noble side to many people, including his parents, and felt upset at the disparity between what he had imagined and the reality. In his disappointment, he tended to exaggerate their negative qualities, much as he had once had exaggerated the positive ones.

In New York, he encountered greater challenges and went through numerous learning phases in his life, meeting key people who solidified his views and beliefs before enjoying the fruits of living in forgiveness. He dropped his defense mechanism and paid deep attention to others. He got rid of his naïve perspective and adopted a more realistic view of life. This involved focusing his attention outward instead of inward and honing the observational and empathic skills that he naturally possessed. This in turn meant moving past his childhood tendency to idealize and demonize people, and seeing and accepting them as they were. He resisted the temptation to interpret what people said or did as somehow implicitly involving him, because he knew this would turn his thoughts inward. He trained himself to pay less attention to the words that people said and paid greater attention to their tone of voice, the look in their eyes, their body language – all signals that might reveal a nervousness or excitement that would not be expressed verbally. If he could get people to become *emotional*, they would reveal a lot more.

As he was standing in his kitchen thinking and worrying about things and people he could not control, he thought of his past and calmed down. He remembered that he did not want anything except what was needed: God's love. He did not expect anything from anyone except God's promises, as he believed that expectations were the root of all delusions and sorrow.

LEVY PARKER

- THE LAWYER -

CHAPTER THREE

"Something old, something new, something borrowed something blue, a silver sixpence inside your shoe."

No one is really sure when this custom started; it is believed by many to have begun during the Victorian era. Nevertheless, couples have honored this custom through the centuries, and even on the day Levy got married. It couldn't have been a more beautiful day to tie the knot.

It was a beautiful summer afternoon in the grandiose botanical garden in the backyard of the Parker mansion, in the Hamptons, New Jersey. The cool breeze was gently tickling the orchard's leaves, making a hissing noise that instigated peacefulness. While the grass was so green that it looked like an artificial lawn, it gave off a refreshing natural earthy smell of newly cut grass. The decorations were simple and light, yet very elegant. All the chairs had white linen with pink and yellow ribbons tied to them. There were flowers everywhere: white and pink roses, white narcissus, orchids, white lilies, pink peonies, carnations and tulips. There was a four-man quartet playing Johann Sebastian Bach's *Largo Ma Non Tanto* next to the altar, where Father Nick was patiently waiting to get his good friend Levy married.

All the guests had dressed to impress, wearing all their fine jewelry, curious-looking hats, tuxedos and designer dresses. They had already sat down and made themselves comfortable, and were anxiously whispering and enviously gossiping as they waited for the bride to appear.

Levy was standing there as nervously as any man would in his situation, smiling anxiously at Father Nick, looking for reassurance as he remembered Nick's words a few months back at church when he was taking his matrimonial sessions with his wife-to-be: *"A person who gives is freed from envy. A person who gives freely is loved by all. It's hard to understand but it is by giving that we gain strength. However, there is a proper way to give, and the person who understands this is strong and wise."*

Nick, looking deep into Levy's eyes, smiled back, giving a quick wink then looking ahead like it was a small thing. The small act of composure rejuvenated Levy's confidence and he stopped fidgeting. Father Nick's look reminded Levy of how far he had come personally and morally to be able to give his all to Annie, and giving his friend Nick the honor of doing so.

You see, Levy was forty-one years old and getting married for the first time. Levy met Nick seventeen earlier in 1996, in a college debate in a philosophy class. Levy was a twenty-four years-old senior, while Nick was just a twenty-two-year-old freshman. They had opposite backgrounds. Levy was a tough kid from rural New Jersey who had grown up in London, Stockholm, Rome, Kyoto and Botswana by the time he was fourteen years old. Nick was a poor boy from Africa who had never left his small town until he lost his whole family in a horrible genocide. After their intense debate, they became instant friends. Levy was moved by Nick's past, while Nick liked the fact that Levy was not ignorant as most Americans were. He knew about the world and Nick wanted to learn from him.

Returning to the States from the time spent in all four corners of the world, Levy became a high-school football star. He used his skills on the gridiron to earn himself a free ride at Princeton. Even though he didn't need it, he made it a personal challenge. Not only was he a jock, but he was book-smart as well. This came naturally, as his father was a wealthy scientist who had worked for the European Commission in Italy three years earlier, investing heavily in an up-coming company called Nokia. He had one older brother, Stan, who was away in Paris trying to sell his works of art.

The day they met, Levy had already lost his scholarship due to his pugnaciousness. He managed to transfer to NYU through his father's influence and was in his senior year of law school. He had been sanctioned for fighting ever since he was a kid, and the behavior followed him until his college years. One fight almost landed him in jail, while other brawls made him lose friends, his reputation and now his scholarship. He got a second chance - literally.

His father warned him while they were wine-tasting in California: "Son" pausing as he lifted his glass and sniffing his red 1991 Bordeaux wine. "Events in life are not negative or positive. They are completely neutral. The universe does not care about your fate; it is indifferent to the violence that may hit you or to death itself. Things merely happen. It is your mind that chooses to interpret them as negative or positive. And because you have layers of fear and insecurity that dwell deep within you, your natural tendency is to interpret temporary obstacles in your path as something larger. Do you understand what I am trying to tell you?" Mr. Parker asked his son as he looked at his wine glass. "*Yes Dad*" Levy answered remorsefully like an eight-year-old boy. "In such a frame of mind son, you exaggerate the dangers and lose control because you perceive everything through the lens of your emotions and your perceived enemies keep winning as you never get to control your situation." Mr. Parker added looking straight into his son's eyes. "I just want to be the best, Dad. I want it bad, and if it is not my reality, I will do everything in my power to change it," Levy answered back with a look of epiphany.

The interesting thing about Levy was that on most days he could be very calm and methodical. He could argue any case or situation with clear and concise words and lots of charisma. However, he tended to be emotional when his ego got hurt due to the fact that he was extremely competitive, jealous and envious of others. These emotions got heightened when it involved people he knew.

Ever since he was young, he always had what he needed, wanted and more. He traveled the world with his family, and he was lucky to see many things, learn different languages and meet people from all four corners of the world. His tastes became refined, and he felt a need to uphold a certain status and reputation. In his mind, he was different. He believed that he was entitled to the best, and he also came to believe that he would automatically become the best at everything he put his mind to do. Being exposed to the world and its injustices, he felt compelled to fight other people's causes even if it didn't affect him directly. But the truth was that it did affect him personally. Thus, he decided that he would be a lawyer. This kind of environment would fuel his extreme competitiveness, soothe his guilt for being privileged, and fill the gap that is constantly empty in most humans: *the purpose-driven life task of doing something meaningful.*

In reality, his feistiness was a hidden confession of inferiority. He always felt discontent over another's superiority over him, whether it was in possessions, talent or good fortune, unless he had provided it or was somehow part of it. He secretly desired others' traits, status, abilities or situation, so he worked hard to get the perfect look, style, gadgets and act - mimicking all the various people he secretly venerated.

His two hundred and thirty pounds of pure muscle intimidated people including his professors. His deep voice and six-foot three frame lifted almost every girl's skirt that he encountered. The minutiae of his personality made him a perfectionist, but also fed his vanity in the sense that he could not be seen unless his matt-black hair was neatly combed backwards and held firmly in place with ounces of gel. He always looked like he had just stepped out of the shower, with Rayban sunglasses on his face, hiding his intense blue eyes. He had a Bretling watch on his wrist, Stacy Adams on his feet, three to four gold and ruby rings on his fingers and Yves Saint-Laurent's Fahrenheit cologne that could be smelled from miles away. Levy was out to prove something - a classical example of narcissism.

The class was called Classical Philosophy - Philo 3301. It was in the middle of the semester, during the cold, windy days of November. The results from the mid-term exams had shown that two students were slightly ahead of the rest of the class. These students were Nick and Levy. Nick had moved out of the Pécresses' penthouse to live alone in Harlem, living on 94th between 2nd and 3rd, part of that unknown shifting border between east Harlem and the rest of Manhattan. He felt that this was where he needed to be in his quest to help those who needed it the most.

He had finished his prerequisite English courses and could speak the language fluently by then. He had officially become a freshman, even though he had been at the university for almost three years at the English center with all the other foreign students. He quickly figured out the American culture and did not find it hard to assimilate with the society. He understood that Americans were extremely independent, which in turn tended to make them individualistic. They had this burning desire to be different from each other, mainly due to their strong belief in freedom of choice. For this reason their culture was venerated by dependent nations and hated by extremist ones. He noticed odd preferences like their inordinate need for 'elbow room': they liked personal space around them. Nick, he never understood the dress code – many people, especially teenagers, wore strange clothes, and many had tattoos and body piercings. Again, the whole notion of freedom of choice was the reason. *What a great nation,* Nick would tell himself whenever he saw things or behavior he did not understand.

This was going to be his third Thanksgiving. He had many things to be thankful for as he mentally prepared for the debate while he was being given his flu shots. To spice things up, Professor Richardson had decided to hold a debate that would account for forty percent of the entire grade for the class.

The topic of the debate was a classic philosophy question: "Can God create a stone so big and heavy that he himself cannot lift?" Professor Richardson was a very curious and pleasant lecturer who was earnestly interested in how his students perceived life. "By a show of hands, how many of you believe or think that there is a God out there?" Prof Richardson asked. About 47 out of 56 students raised their hands. "Ok good. In that case how many of you believe or think that he created the world" he asked again. About 30 students out of 56 raised their hands. "Interesting. One last question, people. By a show of hands, how many of you believe or think that this so called God can create a stone so big and heavy that he himself cannot lift it? Think about it first and then raise your hands, because we are going to have a debate in two weeks and it will basically make up your entire class grade." Prof Richardson finally asked.

The hands rose up slowly. After two minutes or so, fifty students raised their hands. They were asked to prepare their arguments and choose a leader to represent each school of thought, and three speakers for each side. However, there were only six students who did not agree with the statement. They would have a lot of work to do. Levy was one of the six students, while Nick was extremely confused about religion and the thought of a greater being who loved us more than we loved ourselves. This was going to be interesting, Levy thought to himself. "I am going to annihilate them," he vowed to himself. "Especially that African guy who got the highest mark on the mid-term." He looked from a distance at Nick talking to a fellow student.

CHAPTER FOUR

On the day of the debate, everyone in class was nervous. To heighten emotions while balancing objectivity, Professor Richardson had arranged to have it in the main auditorium and invited other students and professors to assist in the debate. He himself would be the moderator and asked two other professors to give points according to the quality and presentation of the arguments. The issue was not to have a right answer but the manner in which the students expressed and defended their side of the debate.

He asked both sides to start with opening statements, and then similar questions would be asked of each, with every person having appropriate time to speak.

Nick was not the leader of the group but was voted to be the main speaker aided by two other students. Levy appointed himself main speaker and automatically became the leader as well. They were just six of them, but the other five students lacked confidence and did not speak much. However, they were very knowledgeable and loyal to their religion and beliefs.

The men wore suits and ties, while the girls looked very professional and elegant as they all sat waiting for Professor Richardson to get things underway. "Welcome, ladies and gentlemen, to our final exam which happens to be a debate. We all thank you for taking the time to come and listen and support your fellow students as they discuss the plausibility of an ultimate omnipotence of a higher being through the question: Can God create a stone so heavy and big that he himself cannot lift it?" - Professor Richardson introducing the debate. "Without further ado, I will let the main speakers present their opening statements."

After the toss of a coin that quickly fell back on its tale, Nick would be first to present the fact that there was no possibility of omnipotence. This was his opening statement: "Most believers - Christians, Catholics, Protestants, Anglicans, Muslims and Jews - follow and worship one God, and this higher being is conceived as the Supreme Being in each religion and worthy of worship because he is uniquely perfect. Nothing greater can be conceived. Whatever qualities 'God' possess, he possesses them to an absolute and ultimate degree. Hence it is not just that 'God' is the greatest conceivable being but rather that, being this being, he must possess all conceivable qualities to the greatest conceivable extent. The three traditional qualities applied to God that stand out are: God is all powerful, (omnipotent), all knowing, (omniscient), and all good (omnibenevolent). It has also been claimed that God's existence must be independent of any other existence distinguishing him from beings of his creation: that he is incapable of experiencing emotions or passions and that he is independent of matter, time and change. However, the application of these attributes raises serious philosophical difficulties, which brings me to today's debate topic: Can God create a stone so big and heavy that he himself cannot lift? This has to do with the attribute of omnipotence. Philosophers call it the paradox of the stone. It is our belief that it appears that this question cannot be answered in a way that is consistent with God's omnipotence. For if we say that God CAN create a rock so heavy that he cannot lift it, then it must be concede that God lacks the power to lift that rock. And if we

DENY that God can create a rock so heavy that he cannot lift it, then it must be conceded that God lacks the power to create that rock. Either way there is something that God cannot do, which highlights the absurdity of notion of omnipotence. Thank you." Nick bowed and walked back to his seat.

The audience clapped and cheered, as Nick was very elegant, articulate and concise. "Straight to the point," one fellow student whispered in his ear as he resumed his seat. As the spectators continued whistling, chanting and applauding, Professor Richardson said: "Thank you, thank you for your enthusiasm, but we have to give way for our opposing speaker and give him the same amount of respect." Levy stood up with lots of confidence and took his place on the podium. As he walked, there were some grunts and whispers from the small crowd, especially from girls, as he was considered a heart breaker/ heartthrob/ player - the typical handsome and envied rich bad boy. He cleared his throat and began. This was his opening statement:"Now that my fellow classmate has explained to everybody what omnipotence means and the attributes most associated with God, it would be futile for me to repeat his well explained understanding of it. But the fact remains that God is all-powerful. But, what does this really mean? I am going to help you think out of the box. I am going to free your mind from narrow thinking.

A variant of the same dilemma is the 'Paradox of Sovereignty', which asks could a sovereign God create a law that binds himself? This basically means that it's not possible for God to be morally flawed because he does not worship anything or anyone – for if God is morally flawless, then presumably there are a number of things he cannot do. For example, committing evil acts, which contradicts the claim that he should be able to do them, being omnipotent. However, he is an omniscient God as well. He is all-knowing. This means that God must know what actions he will or will not perform in the future. Thus the possibility of an impossibility is a contradiction in terms if we adhere to the question whether God can create a stone so heavy and big that he himself cannot lift it. In any event, we construe omnipotence not as the ability to do anything at all but as the power to do only that which is intrinsically possible, which is consistent with God's omnipotence by the fact that he cannot perform a self-contradictory task. He may be able to create the universe and restore the dead to life, but his omnipotence is not compromised if he cannot undo the past. Thankfully he is a God of purpose. What would be the purpose of creating this stone in the first place? He sent his only Son to earth to die for the sins of his creations. I firmly believe that he doesn't need to prove his strength to his creation in this manner. Even if he did, that stone would have to be enormous. He created us in his image. Look at yourselves. Now imagine a stone so big and heavy that you cannot lift it. That stone would have to be about your size. Now if God has to create one his size, it would have to be the size of the whole universe. Thus if the stone is the size of the entire universe, then where would he lift it to? Thank you!

You could hear a pin drop as Levy looked at Nick with a smirk on his face. Nick, being objective, could not help but smile, nodding his head in awe at Levy's opening statement. Levy got a standing ovation as he walked back to his seat next to his five satisfied classmates. The funny thing was that Levy did not even believe in God.

*

Later that day, Levy was at a bar in Tribeca, where most of the wealthy college students hung out. He sat at the counter with a toothpick at the corner of his mouth, very pensive, drinking a Budweiser with a shot of Jack Daniels next to it. His posses, Zack and Michael were on his left, yapping about everything and nothing and acting like fools. It was old school night at Odeon Café. David Bowie's *Let's Dance* was playing in the background. His phone rang. He was one of the few students who owned a Motorola mobile phone at that time. "Speak on it," Levy answered playfully, recognizing his home number. "Hey buddy, how's it hanging?" Stan, Levy's brother answered. "Stan is that really you? You're home? I thought you would be back on Friday. What a pleasant surprise, bro!" Levy replied. "Yeah man. Mom wanted me to come earlier to prepare for Thanksgiving dinner. I got some stuff for you. Don't stay up too late now," Stan laughed mischievously. "Hahaha. I won't. At least not as late as you would. Are you still sober, by the way?" Levy asked. "Ummm. We will talk when you get home. How about that?" Stan added. "I am at Odeon Café. Just come by. I'm celebrating, and I just topped my philosophy class!" Levy exclaimed proudly. "Well I had a long flight and..." Stan began justifying himself when Levy cut him off. "Come on dude, I haven't seen you in what? Six months? Do me this favor, I promise I won't make you drink." Levy interrupted with a tone of false sincerity. "Shoot, whatever. Ok! Ok! I will be there in 20. See you in a bit." Stan hanged up the phone.

CHAPTER FIVE

It was quarter past ten in the evening. Michael Jackson's *Liberian Girl* was playing in the background when Nick and two fellow African students from Ghana came into the bar. They looked like they were freezing by the way their shoulders were shrugged up close to their ears, and were blowing their hot breath into their hands. The barman dropped a shot of Tequila in front of Levy. *"I didn't order this,"* Levy retorted surprised. *"Compliments from the two blondes over there next to the DJ,"* the barman nonchalantly answered, pointing at the girls. Levy looked at them expressionlessly. They looked back lasciviously, lifting their shot glasses and giggling. Levy followed suit, cracking half a smile. "Well done, man," he heard from behind him, feeling a hand gently patting his shoulder. He looked back and noticed Nick naively smiling and waiting for a reaction. "I'm Nick. We haven't officially been introduced." Levy was getting drunk. He looked at Nick without saying a word, his eyes red from alcohol and fatigue, when he finally shook his hands warmly, retorting, "Levy. Nice meeting you buddy."

They exchanged a few pleasantries. Nick was polite and elegant, asking intelligent questions and enthralling Levy with his background and the whole genocide story. Levy told him proudly of his time in Botswana. As they chatted and gabbed about geography, politics and social issues like racism and homosexuality, Stan interrupted them. "What's up guys?"

Everyone was getting tipsy and drunk by then and emotions got a little bit more volatile.

Levy presented his brother Stan to everyone, who talked a bit about his art and the little fame he got for it in lower Manhattan. He amazed Nick with the story of how he found himself in Paris and the kind of lifestyle he was currently living. His childhood best friend from their time in London had relocated to Paris to pursue his career in the catering industry, and this best friend had told Stan in a letter that Paris offered painters an advantage he could not find anywhere else: the museums in which he could study the old masters.

All this wealth of life experiences and ideas was what made Nick tick and feel happy to be alive. Listening and learning new things from people was what Nick believed would make him grow, but most importantly make society as a whole a better place to live in. In any event, this beautiful moment could not last long, as Nick came to understand what made the world go round: man's biggest weaknesses – women and money.

Lucy Hammond and her group of friends entered the bar, and the customers couldn't help but stare at them. She was the only daughter of the one and only Marcus Hammond, co-founder of Hammond & Weisberg Capital. He was a maverick hedge fund investor from Newcastle in the UK. He came to the US in the early seventies looking for his American dream, as he believed that he was ahead of his time for the conservative England. In his earlier years with his partner in crime Carl Weisberg who tragically died in his quest to climb Mount Everest, they revolutionized the dynamics of hedge-funding and made themselves billions of dollars in the process. He married an all-American girl from Philadelphia and had a baby girl named Lucy, but as business picked up, he got caught up in his trade, working up to eighteen hours a day. He forgot about his family, and the couple was divorced after four short years just as the money started pouring in. He got lost in it and remarried twice before settling with a girl the same age as his daughter. He lived in the penthouse of his own thirty -stories building in Manhattan. However, one thing was for sure: he adored his daughter.

*

Lucy was a very attractive, smart girl who knew what she wanted out of life: power. She mingled with everybody but never got attached to anyone. She never put too much trust in her friends, but knew how to use her enemies. Her vanity got the best of her as she understood how much depended on her reputation. She played the power game very well but very subtly, posing as a nice, calm person, but deep down she was ruthless. She was Levy's biggest crush. The confident, intelligent former football star could get any girl he wanted, but could not come to brace himself or think straight when it came to Lucy. However, the interesting part of this story was how Lucy had a soft spot for the talented and passionate Stan Parker.

Levy noticed her arrival as his brother and Nick gabbed about slavery and freedom of the mind. Nick, however, noticed how Levy's composure instantly altered. For the very first time he showed excitement and intrigue, buttoning up his shirt and hiding his gold chain. He removed a tiny comb from his pocket and re-adjusted his hair backwards. He asked the barman for a glass of water and popped gum in his mouth.

Lucy hugged and greeted people as she noticed Stan at the bar. She walked graciously with her curly hair, fit body and amazing smile towards the brothers. She reached Stan and Nick, interrupting their conversation.

"Hey, stranger!" Lucy spoke, gently poking Stan in his ribs, while biting on her lips raising one eye brow. She looked more gorgeous than ever, Levy thought as he realized that she was giving all her attention to his brother. Stan looked back, perplexed, but could not help but smile as he recognized his high school fling. "Well, look at what the cat dragged in! Miss Hammond in the flesh. Don't you look all grown up in that sweater of yours?" Stan replied jokingly, hugging her. They exchanged a few kind and flirtatious words while everybody stared at them. "Do you remember this big fellow right here?" Stan quipped, pointing at his brother. "Are you kidding? Levy! Look at you. You look good, old friend," Lucy answered tactfully, spreading her arms wide open waiting for a hug. Levy couldn't contain himself and just grabbed her in his big arms and lifted her off the ground, making her scream out a tamed sharp sound of joy. They both laughed out loud. "How you doing, Lucy? Haven't seen you since Shawn's party last month." Levy said. "I know I have been M.I.A. lately. I have been doing an internship at my father's firm. All this mixed with classes and assignments... it's hard for me to find time to socialize." Lucy answered.

She was also a NYU student. What Nick didn't know yet was that when the Parkers came back to the US they moved to the Hamptons. Their neighbors were the Hammonds. The boys went to the same high school with Lucy, even carpooled together in the Hammonds' limousine in the mornings going to school. The brothers introduced her to their new acquaintance, Nicholas, and from that moment on, things would never be the same.

Nick, feeling out of place, understood that it was time for him to get out of the way before things got awkward. He and his Ghanaian friends found a small table in the corner lit by a dim yellow bulb where they would be comfortable out of people's view. Lucy took Nick's seat while waving him goodbye. She paused, smiled and looked at Stan almost blushing. "So, tell me everything. What have you been up to?" Lucy asked, engrossed by Stan's presence.

She was consumed with a burning desire for the guy. Women are often deeply oppressed by the role they are expected to play - they are supposed to be the tender, civilizing force in society, wanting commitment and lifelong loyalty - but their relationships often give them a routine and endlessly distracted mate instead of romance and devotion. At first it may seem strange that a man who is clearly dishonest, disloyal and has no interest in marriage would have any appeal to a woman. But throughout all of history, and in all cultures, this type has had a fatal effect. What this man offers is what society normally does not allow women to engage in: an affair of pure pleasure, an exciting brush with danger.

Stan was different from most people: he was free – spirited - free of the constraints of virtue and decency. He exuded a sense of risk and darkness, suggesting that he was rare and thrilling. He was bold, and was all about the expression of emotions in non-verbal ways. He believed that language was limited and that it could not describe all of the soul's beauty and essence. He had a bunch of explicit tattoos in areas of his body that could not be hidden. He had an unorthodox and provocative hairstyle. It looked like an American Indian Mohawk. He never wore a belt; his black pants rolled at the ankles were held by classic suspenders. He wore no socks, with red or orange Dock Martin's depending on his mood. He wore numerous colorful African beads on his wrist, which hissed every time he moved his arm. This was the power of attraction:

whether you liked him or not, you could not help but be intrigued by this type of character.

Lucy and Stan started flirting outrageously, as Levy looked on, growing more and more jealous. He started talking to Zack and Michael, acting like he was not bothered by her peculiar interest in his brother. He believed that his brother was odd and not what women wanted. He ignorantly believed that he had what women desired. He started laughing extra hard at jokes that were not that funny, trying to draw attention towards himself. He really hated it when he was not the center of attention. The more Lucy earnestly giggled at his brother's jokes, the more he got green with envy. He ordered five shots of tequila for each person. The move surprised everyone, especially Stan who looked at his brother with intrigue for his cowardly move. "What's this for now, Lev?" Stan asked, feeling attacked. "Come on, bro, we are celebrating. Can't you see that everybody is happy to see you?" Nick replied, smiling like a conman. "Why not? One drink won't hurt anybody," Lucy cut in, lifting her shot glass and handing another to Stan. Stan's ego was being inflated by all the attention directed his way, and his uncontrollable impulsiveness prompted him to say, "Yeah ok. What the hell." He lifted his shot glass before downing it.

As one drink led to another, everybody got tipsy except for Stan. He really went hard on the drinks. He had been battling an uncontrollable drinking problem, and Levy had aimed deliberately at this weakness. Stan lost touch with reality and started gabbling like a bona fide drunkard. For a moment, Levy thought that his deceitful maneuvers had worked to his advantage but Lucy enjoyed Stan's silliness regardless. She introduced him to her friends and they all had a ball. They started singing karaoke, laughing uncontrollably and dancing like they were the only ones in the bar. All this further enraged Levy, who by then was flirting with the two blondes who had sent him drinks earlier in the evening. He tried to make his brother drink some more, but Lucy noticed what Levy was up to. She pulled Stan away and invited him to go home with her. Stan, excited by what she implied, satiated his thirst instantly and followed her out the bar.

Levy could not believe what had just happened. He had mixed emotions, including a bit of guilt, but then hoped that his brother's drinking problem would spoil whatever chance he had with his dream girl. In a flash, he started imagining them having wild sex. Catching himself thinking unpleasant thoughts, he decided to head home.

As soon as he stepped out of the bar, green with envy and trying to walk straight, he noticed a girl being harassed by a guy just outside the bar. They looked like they knew each other, by the way they were arguing. However, the fellow was being slightly physical and the girl kept yelling at him, telling him to never touch her again and to leave her alone. This was when Levy's natural instinct to help those in unfavorable situations kicked in, and he challenged the low-life with a tough demeanor and confidence, shouting: "Is there a problem here?" Fortunately for the girl, her aggressor was intimidated. The guy looked at her and said: "You are just a little whore anyway." He let go of her, pushing her towards Levy, and quickly walked away. She stumbled, falling flat on her stomach. Levy hurried to her aid while looking at the guy running away, yelling: "You bastard, you better make sure that I never see you again or else I swear will break your face. Coward!" Levy threatened him. "Fuck you!" the assailant replied in the distance.

The young lady started crying as she tried putting

her belongings back in her tiny purse. Levy started helping her and kept telling her that everything was going to be alright. He helped her back to her feet. She had bloody knees from the fall. "You need to get that disinfected" Levy said, noticing her short skirt and beautiful legs. "I'm going to be fine," the young girl replied. "I'm Levy. I just want to help," Levy added. "Thank you. But I will be OK," the young girl retorted. "At least let me drop you home or get you a cab," Levy insisted. She wiped her tears off her cheeks. She calmed down, took a deep breath and looked at Levy's eyes, then cracked a smile with her make-up melting down her face. "I'm sorry. Thank you for helping me. I'm Annie."

They stared at each other as if this was meant to be. For some odd reason they both felt like kissing, but then Levy's friends came out laughing like pure idiots: "I think I should go home." Annie said, walking away from her savior. "How will I make sure that you're going to be alright? I mean, I don't want that creep disturbing you ever again," Levy retorted as she walked towards a cab. "That creep is my step-brother, and if you want to see me again, stop looking at yourself once in a while and you will notice that I am in your e-commerce class," Annie replied, getting into the cab.

Levy felt ashamed as the cab drove away. He felt as if he had a new challenge. Intuitively, he knew that he had stumbled upon something real and meaningful, but it was hard for him to make sense of it all.

A few days later, Levy was eager to go to his e-commerce class. He dressed smartly and casually: no rings, no sunglasses and no gel - just plane khaki trousers and a marine-blue shirt. His hair was slightly curly without the gel. He looked natural.

*

Seventeen years later, as Levy and Annie took matrimonial sessions as required preparations for them to be able to be married in the Catholic Church, Levy found himself alone with Father Nick in his office. He was vulnerable, emotional and ended up talking about his true feelings and his most hidden secrets. He told him of the night at the bar, and what really happened. Until that moment, Father Nick did not know the whole story.

He started by explaining how he met Annie and how he felt as if the universe had sent him a gift or a path towards a more meaningful life. He then divulged how jealous he was of his brother and the obsession he had had with Lucy. He explained how he ruined some of his brother's artwork, rendering him ineligible for certain key exhibitions that would have put him on the right track in his career. He also admitted that on the night he cheated on Annie with Lucy just to spite his brother and feel good about himself. He always had to win, no matter how he did it.

Lucy had come to Levy's apartment distraught and sad one evening, crushed by the fact that Stan was actually in love with another girl he had met in Paris. That same night at the bar, Stan and Lucy had gone back to her apartment to enjoy themselves. Stan, being drunk, kept talking of this girl and mistakenly called her name out during their sexual encounter. This shattered Lucy's ego. Hurt and out to get even, she went to Levy to make sure that Stan would regret his mistake for the rest of his life. She undressed and asked Levy to make love to her like no man had ever done. The news got back to Stan through Levy, but orchestrated by Lucy. It crushed him. Stan later learned from art dealers how Levy was the person behind his failure in his endeavors as an aspiring artist. Stan was an extremely emotional soul, and for a long period could not believe all he had heard. He felt betrayed and got lost deeper in his alcoholism. He sought refuge in new and more potent drugs, and one day he got so high that he bought a ticket and went back to Paris leaving a letter to his mom explaining the whole situation. He lamented on the fact that his father and Levy only wanted his failure for them to prove their point. He vowed that he would never come back.

The brothers never spoke to each other again, bringing so much sorrow to their mother that it inevitably ruined her relationship with the other two men in her life.

That day, in Father Nick's office, Levy confessed sincerely and looked for some kind of divine salvation. Ever since he was a child, Levy admired others, especially his older brother. As he grew up, this admiration turned inwardly, where he wanted others to covet his possessions, looks and manner. But most importantly, he wanted others to want to be like him. Coveting may indeed be one of the virtuous vices of a competitive economy, but there is nothing virtuous about envy. Coveting says: *"He has it; I want it"*. Envy, though, says: *"If I can't have it, nobody can."*

At that point Nick understood that to an envious man nothing is more delightful than another's misfortune, and nothing more painful than another's success. The vice of envy is always a confession of inferiority. Ironically, it is also the only sin that no one ever confesses. People often confuse it with jealousy or interchangeably use both words trying to describe the same feeling. However, jealousy is an emotion felt toward people and relationships. On the other hand, envy is a negative emotion felt due to comparison with one's own possessions. Jealousy originates from a positive attachment to another, while envy stems from resentment and begrudgment. The components underlying envy include feelings of inferiority, ill will and possibly guilt or denial.

An envious person views the well-being of others with distress, even though it does not detract from one's own. It is a reluctance to see our own well-being overshadowed by another because the standard we use to see how well off we are, is not the intrinsic worth of our own well-being. Envy aims, at least in terms of one's wishes, at destroying others' good fortune. It is a frustrated desire turned destructive. Envy is what leads a child's to break another child favorite toy, or a boss to sabotage a talented employee.

Watching Levy cry remorsefully for his wickedness, Farther Nick gently explained that the world operates according to a well-regulated system that allows for no error, accidents, chance or luck. Nothing happens by chance. Every occurrence has its cause, from which it follows by necessity because nothing can exist without cause. Every person's good fortune will always be earned and justified in some way or another. Whatever comes into your life, whether good or not to your taste, all happens as a reaction to your past Karma. As the old adage states, what you sow, you will have to reap. When we are grateful for the good we already have, we attract more good into our life, and envy is an expression of ingratitude because by acknowledging the good that is already in your life, it is simply the most basic foundation for all abundance.

Levy and Annie got married on July 7th 2012 and now have a healthy baby boy called Stan Jr.

STAN PARKER

- THE ARTIST -

CHAPTER SIX

The distant sound of the ambulance woke Stan up; disturbing his deep sleep. *Where am I?* he asked himself, opening his bulging eyes painfully.

He looked to his left, noticing a beautiful semi-covered naked butt. He slowly looked to his right and saw another well-rounded naked posterior. He smiled proudly, not remembering what exactly had happened for him to wake up between two gorgeous women. He lifted his upper body with much agony to scout his surroundings, letting out low grunt. There was some light peeping through a crack in the drapes, which looked expensive. It was a large room. He saw lots of clothes thrown around on the marble floor, recognizing his black Armani trousers. There were a bunch of high heels next to the door, and a line of fine white powder with a neatly rolled fifty-Euro note next to it, on what looked like the hard cover of a children's book. Cocaine! *The irony*, he thought to himself, letting out a sadistic laugh.

He licked his lips, suffering from a dry throat. "Aherrrm" he cleared his throat, waking up the first girl. "Aheerrmmmmm" he cleared his throat again, louder, waking up the second girl. Their hair was all messed up but they still looked gorgeous. They looked at each other and smiled as if they had stolen cookies out of the cookie jar before dinner.

It had been five years since Stan had seen his family, let alone the USA. He still couldn't forgive his loved ones. He had become bitter, stressed and irritable, which in turn weakened the little self-control he had. He lived a rollercoaster life with constant highs and lows. He acted purely on impulse, neglecting any commitments, but his ego couldn't allow him to show it. He tried hard to suppress it, but it came out in subtle instances like his road rage or lack of concentration in his artwork. If he managed to finish a project, it would be dark or sad. However, his work was captivating, intense, hypnotizing and stylish. But he was never happy with his work - something was always missing, and the smallest details had to be tweaked even if it meant restarting the whole project from scratch. Most of his collections were shelved in his attic, collecting dust.

Because he believed that everyone was against him, he managed to engage himself in unnecessary petty arguments with various people - the cashier at the stores, or a waitress at a restaurant – which drained him emotionally. He even got irritated by small kids or toddlers - the most innocent of creatures.

He slept a lot and drank uncontrollably, especially at odd hours of the day. He smoked reefer at least five times a day, occasionally snorted cocaine - smack, booger sugar, white girl. Whatever you want to call it. He hung around night clubs on most nights of the week, going home with a different girl most times. Degeneration! He would indulge himself in anything that numbed the pain and sadness.

However, the only good thing going for him was the fact that he had his perceived love of his life on his side. Her name was Camille - The French girl he kept talking about when he was with Lucy. She brought him everything that he wanted in terms of his understanding of companionship. She was free-spirited, spontaneous and fun, and she did not care about people's opinion of her. He gladly found refuge in her social acumen and connections. He adored her wit and her seductive ways. She looked like a model, with her petite body, her red lips, her funky blonde hair and her hazel eyes. He was infatuated. They held hands every where they went, kissed sporadically in public and had impromptu sex in public toilets. But the truth was that she was only attracted by the idea of him. She wanted to live a fairytale. She had a tough upbringing surrounded by supremacist doctrines and ideologies. He was a foreigner, a wealthy American and a true artist. In her mind, he embodied the exact opposite of what she was made to believe and value.

When they met six years ago, he showed a lot of promise and looked like he knew where he was going. Sadly, things were not the same. She could intuitively sense that something was really wrong, disrupting his balance. She stayed with him just because she was graced with a natural gift of patience. She never really got worked up over things, but deep down, she still had a tiny ounce of hope.

*

Jane Parker made the effort to communicate with her son on a monthly basis, but his mood swings and tantrums made it hard for her to get her message through to him. Stan's mother was wise, poised and nurturing. It was clear that her son needed a helping hand and guidance in order for him to be successful in his craft. If she somehow managed to succeed in her endeavor, then he would automatically be happy in his life. That was how simple Stan was. "Some people will always need help. Doesn't mean they are not worth helping," she kept telling her husband.

His success would change the whole dynamic of their relationship, but there was another issue: the mistrust and hatred Stan had for his brother and father. "The only way he is going to be able to achieve his goals is if some way he could earnestly overcome his hate in some way," Mrs. Parker told Nick about her worries for her son.

He demonstrated the three main components that make up hate. The first was the steady avoidance of interaction with the people he did not like, which lead to having few facts and little understanding of each other. The second was the strong emotional reaction of passionate anger, contempt and disgust for his family. The third was that he created in his mind a belief system that added to the hot emotions and justified his hate and his firm commitment to avoiding, denouncing and degrading his brother and father.

Mrs Parker was on a mission to support her son because her husband did not give him the benefit of the doubt. He wanted his son to be an engineer or an architect, and believed that he was a failure. "At least if he got married it would make him responsible," he kept telling his wife in bed before falling asleep. He particularly did not like his son's art and was very verbal about it to make his point.

At the beginning of Stan's career, about ten years earlier, he got a few positive recognitions for his art. It went to his head. He was just twenty years old and sold five of his paintings at his first exhibition. He believed that he was a genius, but in reality he was a late bloomer. His goals were imprecise, and his procedure tentative and incremental. This meant that he rarely felt that he had succeeded, and his career was consequently often dominated by the pursuit of a single objective that seemed to never be achieved. He tended to repeat himself in his work, painting the same subject many times and gradually changing its treatment in an experimental process of trial and error. He rarely made specific preparatory sketches or plans for a painting. He considered the production of a painting as a process of searching in which he aimed to discover the image in the course of making it. He typically believed that learning was a more important goal than making a finished painting. He was a perfectionist and was plagued by frustration his inability to achieve his goal.

Jane Parker believed that her son was just not capable of dealing with all these issues by himself. Although he was simply immature and extremely emotional, his raw talent and passion was unmatched. Nevertheless, if it was tamed and focused in the right direction, he could achieve something unimaginable. She decided to create a dream team and accepted the fact that she would have to be cunning, shrewd and very subtle in her ways. She reckoned that the best way to help her son was through forbearance and blind faith.

First he would need a patron. That word has a condescending edge to it today, because we think it far more appropriate for artists to be supported by the marketplace. But the marketplace, which worked for people like Picasso or Monet, whose talent were so blindingly obvious that an art dealer offered them unimaginable stipends the minute they got to Paris. She would secretly be paying his bills through a decoy - an old acquaintance of hers from Brooklyn who would falsely appear to be in love with Stan's work and show faith in his abilities. He would be secretly working as a spy for Jane Parker, giving her information about of Stan's progress.

The second part of her plan was to make sure that Camille stayed at his side. This was imperative. She managed to get hold of her, befriended her and talked to her once every two months - without Stan's knowledge, of course. She had the perfect motherly words, and got interested in Camille's life and tried to help her as much as she could. Oddly enough, Camille found her gestures endearing.

She then stretched her hand out to his childhood best friend Alistair Peckham from their days in London. Alistair was the only Brit who had managed to garner the coveted three Michelin stars for his high-end restaurant in France. Back in London in the late 1980s, he went into cooking school for he did not have enough patience for hypothetical and idealistic school work. His ultimate goal was to become a professional rugby player, but he had heart problems that prevented him from pursuing his ultimate boyish dream. The difference between Jane's son and Alistair was pragmatism and realism. Alistair ended up working long hours in different premier Michelin-starred kitchens like *Le Gavroche*, *La Tante Claire* in Chelsea and *Harvey's*. He applied himself quietly to his craft, never complained, and learned fast. He quickly became a reliable asset in each of these exquisite establishments. Aware of his excellence, he humbled himself. He wanted to learn more and surpass all his peers. He decided to go to the melting pot of the gastronomic world: Paris.

There he found himself in a foreign country, friendless and penniless, and to make matters worse, he could not speak the language. He was there based on merit. The Paris kitchens were different and tougher. The chefs moved faster and the brigades were bigger. He found himself working for a lower wage and was treated as an apprentice by the other chefs, but he sailed through by working step by step, slowly attaining mastery. Before he realized it, he was working the hard stations like the fish or meat sections. You had to be completely trusted by the head chefs to be on those stations.

In just under just five years, he was sous-chef at

Guy Savoy's restaurant in Paris at the tender age of twenty-seven. After ten years of patience, learning and practice, he ventured on his own near Versailles in 1998 opening his own restaurant *Rose Bonbon*. He got his first Michelin star at the end of the first year of operation, another in 2000 and the third in January of 2001. He was just thirty years old, the youngest chef to do so in the history of the Michelin Guide.

They decided that he was going to be Stan's guardian, protector and coach. He contacted Stan and met up. Stan obviously looked up to him, and Alistair knew how to psych him up. He was going to show him how to work with discipline.

Around the same time, Nick had already published his book. It was quickly and unexpectedly becoming a bestselling novel, and he simultaneously occupied a promising job as a professional counselor at Hammond & Weisberg Capital. He got his break through the help of none other than Lucy, with whom he was becoming close. He got the job just in time, as the company had lost vast amounts of money in the 1999 NASDAQ crash. Most of the twenty-three employees that made up the company needed psychological counseling.

Nick had become close with the Parkers through his friendship with Levy, who was working for the district attorney at the time. Levy's father helped Nick publish his book, working as his manager. He told them of his plans of going back to Burundi to find closure and meet his long-lost cousin who had moved back to the country with her husband. Jane Parker urged Nickolas to pass through Paris on his way to talk to Stan as a desperate move. Nick did not find any reason not to. He had nothing to lose. Better yet, he would visit Paris in the process.

At 3am on September 6th 2001, Jane Parker received a phone call from her spy, who posed as Stan's patron.

He sounded distraught:

"Allo, Jane can you hear me?"

"Yes, slow down, slow down. Calmly tell me what's going on."

"It's bad Jane. He crashed"

"What? Who crashed? Tell me what's going on?

"I'm calling from the hospital. Stan overdosed on cocaine. I luckily found him right in the nick of time and rushed him to the emergency room. He's been stabilized but he's unconscious for the moment."

"Dear God, I'm taking the next available flight out there."

"No, no. Don't do that. It wouldn't be a wise move. He is vulnerable and needs time to rest on his own. I promise I will handle it. It's not about you. It's Camille. She left him. She has been seeing some another guy these last few months."

"My son needs me."

"Trust me on this one, he would not make it if he is aware that you saw him like this. I will handle it"

"I will send Nick then"

"Who is Nick?"

"The shrink!"

CHAPTER SEVEN

Nick got greeted by a tall, lanky and pale gentleman. The fellow had an unmistakable, thick Brooklyn accent. He had bad teeth and smelled of menthol cigarettes and coffee. "Your first time in Paris?" the man asked, picking up Nick's bags. "Thank you. Yes, it is. I'm feeling very privileged at this particular moment. I would have never thought that one day I would be in Paris. It seems like a dream. I'm Nick." The orphan boy stretched his arm to greet the stranger. "Collin, Collin Fishburn. Welcome to the city of lights." The man put the unlit cigarette in his mouth while switching the bag to his left arm, shaking Nick's hand with his right.

As they drove out of the airport, Nick couldn't help but get excited. It was Paris for crying out loud! He always watched movies set in the touristic capital with his younger brothers and dreamt about visiting the place. He had teary eyes as he thought of his siblings being burned alive while he was there, being driven around in one of the most popular cities in the world. He wondered why some people always had a helping hand while others' dreams and plans never reached fruition no matter how much work, patience and passion they put into it. Who made that decision? Who and what was that helping hand? His philosophical thoughts got interrupted by Collin's questions. "So you're a shrink huh?" Collin asked with passive aggression. "You may say so." Nick replied with a big smile on his face. "Well you look like a twelve-year-old. How do you know the Parkers?" Collin asked again. "How do YOU know the Parkers? I thought we were here for Stan?" Nick asked back. "Right, right. Jane told me that you have to meet Alistair. Well, his restaurant is closed tomorrow night. You can rest today and meet up tomorrow. How does that sound?" Collin suggested. "Sounds like a plan," Nick retorted. "Where are you spending the night?" Collin asked. "George V" Nick answered. "Are you kidding me? Whose idea was that?" Collin asked with a surprised look on his face. "Mrs. Parker." Nick retorted.

They drove in silence the rest of the way. Mindful of the task ahead in terms of counseling Stan, he could not focus quite yet. His mind started drifting into childhood fantasies. The first thought that came to his mind was that of Jim Morrison, simply because his grave is in Paris. His mind constantly thought of unimportant facts like these. He started imagining walking up the Eiffel Tower, meandering inside the *Louvre*, and sipping on some old wine along the Champs Élysées just before standing in between the arches of the Arc de Triomphe.

The next day, Nick suggested that Collin, Alistair and himself meet up at the Saint-Germain-des Prés, an iconic bistro where classic French novelist Albert Camus spent most of his time debating with philosopher and author Jean-Paul Sartre or write letters to René Char. They were some of his favorite writers and thinkers. There they would discuss how to handle Stan's predicament. Their meeting was supposed to take place at 6pm, but on that fateful day, the world forever changed because of what happened to France's transatlantic neighbor.

Nick was in his hotel room getting ready to step out when he became glued to his TV screen. He watched as the day enfolded in a tragedy so profound that no one was prepared to witness it. The north tower fell first, as hundreds of firefighters, police officers, medical personnel, construction workers and others scrambled all over the twin towers in New York, trying to do their best to handle a very confusing situation. Just when we thought we had seen the worst, a second plane crashed into the south tower, all in full view of the entire world, in real time. It was the biggest statement anyone had ever made in recent history.

September 11, 2001, was a day of unprecedented shock and suffering in the history of the US. The nation and the world were frighteningly unprepared. One question lingered secretly in everybody's mind: how did this happen?

*

In a serendipitous, sadistic and opportunistic eureka moment, Nick reckoned that in order for Stan to rekindle and make his art meaningful, he would have to alter Stan's concept of creativity by making him see things from a new angle.

Nick's thoughts created ambivalent feelings inside him. He felt as if he was manipulating a child, but he also concluded that Stan was not focusing his energy on the right task. You see, true creativity involves the entire self, emotions, levels of energy, character and the mind. Stan had to invent something that connected with the public.

To fashion a work of art that is meaningful, inevitably requires time and effort. It also entails years of experimentation, various setbacks, failures and the need to maintain a high level of focus. What was imperative was to choose the right task to direct his creative energy. He was going to tap into the

September 11 events.

Nick deduced from Stan's recent past and information given to him by his mother that the guy was hurting bad. He intuitively felt that the feelings of betrayal, sabotage, envy and the recent loss of his perceived love of his life had weakened him almost to the point of suicide. However, this weakness could also be the key to any revival, and turned into a strength. What Stan was not aware of, was that he had done most of the grueling work: the learning, the mistakes, moving to Paris on his own to learn from the greats and the experimentations. Nick believed that the only issue that stunted Stan's progress was that Stan spent too much time entangled in emotional issues, and never quite had enough detachment to reflect and learn from his past experiences. If he managed to use his past experiences and channeled all those feelings deep within him without worrying about what others might think, then all this directed energy would be reflected in his work and the public would automatically feel it and connect.

The whole idea was to tap into the power of context. In reality, if you pay good attention to the trends, ideas, innovative technologies, successful people, timeless movies, riveting novels, hypnotizing art, etc., you will notice that they are all created by people who did not act for their fundamental, intrinsic reasons or who lived in their own world. They were created by people who were acutely sensitive to their environment, who were alert to all kinds of cues, and were prompted to create based on their perception of the world around them. The September 11 events would be the right avenue for Stan, as these horrendous events would eventually bring about an atmosphere, aura and mind-set of hate, anger, vendetta, fear, alienation and grief from loss of loved ones. All these feelings were not unknown to

Stan. It would be perfected, as these feelings would be portrayed and manifested in everyday life.

The next day, they travelled to the outskirts of Paris to go meet Stan who was by then recuperating at Alistair's villa. It was a very quiet, secluded and a peaceful place hidden by trees and shrubs. To Nick's surprise, Stan was very receptive to his presence. He had a photographic memory, and remembered faces easily. Nick also had an aura of serenity and a calmness that immediately put people at ease. Things were already going well so far.

They all sat in the Victorian style living room, and were served tea by a very short maid with tiny eyes. She must have been from the French Polynesian islands. They started talking about the September 11 events to break the ice. After a while, Collin and Alistair decided to have some wine and cheese in the garden. Nick remained in the living room with Stan, who although calm did not make any eye contact. One of his eyes was still blood-shot. He looked thin and slightly pale. He had a few bruises on his neck, but from the looks of it, he was going to be fine. Nick looked straight at him in silence. Stan kept looking around until he noticed some items that made him crack half a smile. There were pictures of Alistair all over the living room, immortalizing his numerous achievements and memorable events. "Do you know I started painting thanks to Alistair?" Stan broke the silence. "When we were younger, he could draw so well. He could draw almost anything. I envied him so much, so I started drawing in secret. I tried so hard to draw like him. My drawings were horrible, so I decided to draw things that I loved and understood. I found refuge in the Incredible Hulk. He embodied everything that I was then." Stan said fixating his eyes on Alistair's pictures. "Really? The Hulk? Do you still see yourself as the Hulk" Nick asked with such integrity in his voice. "I admire him. Bruce Banner is such a nice guy, socially reserved who does not want any trouble. He is in love with a woman he cannot be with due to his sickness. But when angered, he becomes invincible." Stan answered candidly. "Do you feel powerful when you get angry?" Nick asked with stern voice. "I don't know. Why are you here Nick? Did my mother send you here to ask me all these questions?" Stan answered avoiding a straight answer. "I am here because I wanted to visit Paris as I am on my way to my home country to find answers. I presume you know I lost my entire family during the war. I have been all alone ever since. I wish I could tell you how much I miss them, but I am not going to bore you with that. Don't you miss your family?" Nick asked. There was a brief moment of tense silence, when the tiny soft-spoken maid came in asking if they needed any more refreshments. They gracefully declined.

"It's really beautiful outside. Don't you want to get some fresh air?" Nick asked.

"Yeah, why not?" Stan replied.

They joined Collin and Alistair in the garden, where there was a small pond with ducks in it. Alistair and Stan started reminiscing on good old times as Collin told tales of his time in the army during the Iraq '*desert storm*' war. It got quite late in the evening when Nick decided to head home. For the next week, Nick visited Stan every day. They went out in the city, ate at small bistros, went on boat rides and sat in parks in silence yet feeling comfortable with each other's presence. Stan couldn't help but open up. Nick never judged. People always felt like expressing themselves, when they spent time with the orphan.

Stan divulged how insecure he was, becoming dependent on Camille's adoration. She made him feel good about himself. As soon as her attention was on something or someone else, he felt left out and betrayed. She would then be bewildered and unable to relieve his pain because the problem was inside him: his self-doubt.

Nick told him how confused he was with how his life had turned out. He outlined his own insecurities, his pain and the hidden hatred he had for the people who managed to find the power and will to actually burn and kill hundreds of people based on their ethnicity. Nick explained how the way we dealt with stress, disappointment and frustration determines the essence of our personality. He further explained how anger is a feeling we all encounter from time to time. Frequently, we experience it as a response to frustration, hurt, disappointment or repeated hostile fantasies. It is a strong emotion, excited by a real or imagined injury, and is often accompanied by a desire to take revenge, or to obtain satisfaction from the offending party. It begins in folly and ends in repentance. If a person often becomes irritable at trifling things very often, it is a definite sign of mental weakness. An easily irritable person is always unjust. He is swayed by impulses and emotions. Self-restraint or self-control is a sign of great mental strength.

Alone in his luxurious hotel room, Nick pondered the whole concept of anger and how it may do more harm than any other emotion. He realized that the cause of sin or wrong action is desire. Anger is only a modification or form of desire, while anger is desire itself. When desire is not gratified, the person becomes angry at those who stand as obstacles in the path of fulfillment. The sad truth is that anger is personal and the outcome of greed and selfish motives. It has to do with the inability to meet unrealistic, unplanned and impatient expectations – whether our own or those who have expectations of us. We use anger to blame others for our own shortcomings, to justify oppressing others, to boost our own sagging egos, to conceal other feelings and to handle other emotions such as fear – we become more aggressive when we are afraid. This underlying emotion is related to a perceived loss of control over factors affecting our integrity, our beliefs and how we feel about ourselves.

Most people use different terms to describe this emotion: wrath, anger, resentment. Well, the difference is that anger is a sudden sentiment of displeasure. Resentment is continued anger, while wrath is a heightened sentiment of anger. At this point, you could call it rage or fury. Anger is momentary madness. You will not be punished for your anger; you will be punished by your anger, because when a man is under the sway of anger, he will commit all sorts of sinful deeds. He loses his memory, his understanding becomes clouded and his intellect gets perverted. He becomes emotional and impulsive. He will say anything he likes; he will do anything he likes. A hot word results in fighting and stabbing. He commits murder – he himself does not know what he is exactly doing.

*

On their way to the airport, the four of them rode in Collin's car, where Nick kept talking about how worried he was about the state of the world and just how widespread hostility was. Yes, great atrocities were attributed to crazed men like Hitler, Stalin or terrorists such as Bin Laden, but he lamented on how ordinary people could rather easily become evil enough to discriminate against, hurt, and brutalize others or especially themselves.

Nick secretly hoped that his time spent with Stan

would inspire him to let go of all neediness and tap into the power of context and create. Because that was the only way Stan would ever be happy.

Fortunately, that is what he did. He got inspired. Shortly after Nick's departure, Stan threw out most of the stuff in his house: the bongs, the whisky bottles, his old paintings, his sofa and the pictures of him and Camille. He cleaned his house almost to the point of emptying it. He placed a single canvas in the middle of his apartment. He painted a riveting work of art in just three days. It was a close-up of a single hand with a frightening whole in it as if a huge nail had gone through it. He called it *The cleansing of Sin.*

NELLIE DOMORI

-THE RELATIVE-

CHAPTER EIGHT

The humidity gave Nick a shortness of breath. The heat was unbearable and could instantly be felt as soon as he stepped out of the plane. *I will not run, I will not run*, Nick kept telling himself. *I will not cry, I will not cry*, he thought as he hit the tarmac at Bujumbura International Airport; after what seemed like an endless flight of steps down the airplane stairwell. It was about two weeks after the September 11 terror attacks in New York.

He remembered the fateful night of October 1993. He felt a bit of anger but put those feelings aside for the time being as he entered the tiny airport.

It was empty compared to JFK. or Roissy Charles De Gaulle in Paris, and very small. There were a few Europeans with UN passports, and other Burundian teenagers that dressed like kids back in the US; sagging pants and durags on their heads. They looked happy and excited, but arrogant. After filling out the official forms and picking up his bags, he was harassed by people he didn't know, who kept asking him what he had brought them. He graciously declined their request. He was shocked by their audacity and lack of shame. If only he really understood what they went through everyday, maybe he would have better answers- or better yet, a solution. But those were not things he thought about yet.

As he stepped out into the arrivals hall, he stood in front of a big crowd, who kept waving at him. For a moment he thought they were waving at him, then someone behind him would come out running, full of emotions and tears and falling into their loved one's arms with screams of joy. *What a feeling this must be*, the orphan boy thought. All of a sudden he saw a familiar face: a very beautiful woman approaching him with open arms as she spoke in French. "Nickolas? Nico – it's you!"

Nick froze with emotions. He dropped his bags and smiled almost up to his ears, recognizing his mythical cousin from the pictures she sent with her emails. They embraced as she cried with happiness.

*

Nellie's and Nick's grandmothers were sisters, and she was the only relative that he had left. She had gone back to Burundi after sixteen years living abroad in Belgium. She got married there and had a son. Frits, her husband, was fifteen years her senior and had been married once before. He was a chemist from Belgium and they decided to relocate to Burundi, as he found peace there, in the midst of all the chaos going on in the country.

*

The drive to their home was an emotional one for Nick. It had been eight years since he last saw his native country, and he felt a mess of emotions; fear and confusion. It felt like a healthy tooth being yanked out without any anesthesia. Everything had happened so fast, and he hadn't been prepared for the events that occurred. Just like that, he was thrown into the woods to fend for himself. The love and support the Pécresse's gave him was too pure for him to fathom.

It was really hot and humid. He kept sweating. He had rarely spent time in the capital city back when he still lived with his parents, but not much had changed in eight years. Actually, almost nothing had changed. The potholes in the roads eight years ago were still there. Some were even bigger. There was an air or atmosphere of despair, abandonment, negligence and surrender. Things were not going well in the country, but at least they were slightly better than when he left.

How beautiful is this country!, Nick told himself as he looked around like a tourist in his home country, noticing the not-so-distant hills on one side and the lake on the other. Nellie gabbed and gossiped about people they knew, while Nick rolled down the window to smell the lake. He closed his eyes and had a flashing memory of his younger brothers laughing and giggling when they all took a bath together. Frits interrupted his flashback. "So what do you do now that you finished college?" Frits asked, looking at Nick from the mirror, trying to focus on the road. "I'm a counselor at a hedge fund firm in Manhattan," Nick replied. "Interesting. How old are you? You seem to be young to be a counselor. You must be a star," Frits added. "I don't know if I'm a star. All I know is that I feel and understand people. I guess it's just a gift. I'm very grateful. I just turned twenty-seven last month." Nick answered. "Good for you, young man. It would even be better if you could work your magic here. People need counseling here more than you would imagine," Frits added. "You don't say!" Nick retorted rather sarcastically. "So do you love what you do?" Nellie joined in the conversation. "I actually do. I used my conversations for the basis of a book I just finished writing. It just got published. It is actually getting good reviews as we speak, and I just got offered a full scholarship for grad school at Harvard." Nick said proudly. "Really? Wow, Nick! I'm so proud of you. You keep amazing me, cousin. What is the book about?" Nellie asked. "I have a copy with me. Read it and tell me what you think." Nick answered. "I guess we have so much to talk about. I'm honestly glad you are here," Nellie added.

They arrived at their house, a villa in the hills with a view of the whole city. It was astoundingly beautiful. After setting his bags down, he presented them with some gifts: a Cartier watch and Channel No°5 perfume for Nellie, a Mont Blanc pen for her husband, and a Yankee cap, a basketball and CD player for their ten-year-old son Stephane.

Nellie gave him a brief tour of the house as she told him the story of how she met Frits in Brussels. After that he got acquainted with his room. He sat on the bouncy bed, still not fully grasping the fact that he was back in his native country. He took a refreshing shower and went downstairs to be with his cousin. His nose and ears were still congested from the twelve hour flight from Paris. "Eight hours from N.Y to Paris. I spent 2 weeks in Paris, then another ten from Paris to Nairobi. Then two to reach here," Nick lamented.

They sat in the living room, reminiscing on the good old times, and talking about their parents and other departed siblings. She showed him photo albums after photo album. It was a very endearing moment for Nick, who for the first time in a very longtime felt like he belonged somewhere. In a way, this trip would help him move forward. It would not be closure, but an acceptance of reality.

Frits and Stephane joined them only for a few minutes just to let them know that they were leaving for the rest of the afternoon. Stephane needed to attend to his Judo class. "We will see you later!" Frits shouted out of the window of the Range Rover.

As soon as they left, Nellie asked Nick if he wanted to drink something or if he was hungry. Nick gracefully declined, as the jetlag was kicking in. Nellie called for the house help and sent him to buy some drinks.

Nellie was extremely pretty, with very smooth, hairless skin, small pointy nose and a smile to die for. She had put on a few pounds around the waist area and oddly always looked tired with her irresistible puppy eyes. But it gave her charm. As soon as the house help returned with the drinks in a green plastic bag with Sylvester Stallone as Rambo on it, she asked Nick if he was sure he did not want anything. Nick excused himself and went to bed to have some rest.

Waking later, he opened his eyes slowly and immediately felt lost. Blank white walls were all he could see; musty and humid air was all he could feel. The small fan was at full speed but could only barely alleviate the heat. Nick yawned, popping his right ear. He was feeling much better, and hungry.

He ran down the stairs to see what was happening downstairs. The sun was setting, and felt rejuvenated by the breath of cooler air coming in from the wide open glass front doors. As he reached the living room, he saw two empty big brown bottles of Amstel beer on the coffee table. He noticed Nellie's red shoes on the carpet next to the sofa. He made his way to the kitchen, hoping to find her there. He met the house help Juvenal.

"Where is Mrs Nellie?" Nick asked.

"Madame is by the pool at the back. She told me to let her know as soon as you woke up. I have prepared some food for you." Juvenal answered.

"What did you make for me I'm hungry," Nick retorted quite joyfully, noticing yet another empty Amstel bottle.

"Some roast beef, plantain bananas, rice, beans and some lenga lenga." Juvenal quickly responded. Nick didn't pay attention to what Juvenal was saying, as he was looking out through the kitchen window at Nellie on her cell phone.

"So are you going to eat?" Juvenal asked, getting irritated.

"Lenga lenga, you say, huh? The last time I had lenga lenga, I was a small boy. Anyhow, no beef for me, but lots of lenga lenga." Nick answered, walking towards Nellie.

Nellie was on the phone talking loudly, laughing erratically with a cigarette in her left hand between her index and middle finger. A small bottle of gin was in front of her, but Nick could not see any tonic or juice. She drank it straight, with lots of ice. It shocked him a bit, but he would not comment quite yet. She hung up the phone, and she stood up happily, stumbling a bit and holding herself to the chair so that she would not fall. She hugged him for a minute or so saying, "You're up, American boy. I am so happy you are here, cousin. We are going to have so much fun."

They sat back down, and she yelled at Juvenal to bring his food quickly. "It's so hard to find good house help here, you know". She yelled again at Juvenal to bring some lemon.

"I was talking to Chantal, my best friend here. Her husband has traveled. So we are going out to the club tonight. Are you up for it?" Nellie asked as she took a good swig of her gin, munching on the ice as she waited for an answer. "I thought we would do such things later in the week. You know I just travelled from the US," Nick answered, trying to put some sense into the conversation. "Come on, man. Don't be a pussy. How old are you now? You're not a baby anymore. Let's have fun. Live life to the fullest, you know Anyway, you will have time to sleep later. When you're dead!" Nellie retorted, laughing uncontrollably.

It was hard for Nick to find any humor in what she

was saying. For a minute, he did not recognize his cousin. This was another person all of a sudden. *Why did she have to use words like 'pussy'?* he asked himself. He found it vulgar. *Where is all this coming from?*, he pondered.

He agreed to go out to see where all this would lead to. He ate, filling up his stomach, while Nellie ordered Juvenal to bake a cake for him. They chatted until sundown, when she got a phone call from Frits. Her husband and son were on their way back. She told Nick that they had to leave or else it would be difficult for them to go out. She told Juvenal to hide all the ash trays, return all the empty bottles and not say a word to her husband. As far as he knew, they were going to see some old friends.

About five minutes later, Chantal was honking at the gate. They hurried to her car and left the house. In the car Nellie introduced her cousin to her best friend, who had just dropped her husband to the airport. Pleasantries were exchanged. Chantal then opened the glove box, removing a medium sized Gordon gin bottle. The women laughed naughtily, but the only thing Nick kept thinking was, *where is all this coming from? How is this going to end? I bet someone is going to get hurt.*

CHAPTER NINE

They decided to start off the evening with a few drinks at a charming place just by the lake called *Cercle Nautique*. There, they would meet up with other Diaspora Burundians who had come back to the country for various reasons. Nick got introduced to her friends, who all acted and talked like Nellie. They were inebriated, gossiped about other people, judging them, mocking the ones that seemed weak and talked highly of themselves.

Nick had two glasses of wine, but in reality he could not stand alcohol. It affected him badly and quickly, impairing his judgment. He hated being in a situation where he could not think straight, and waking up without a clear head. He decided to get some air and get away from the crowd. Nellie noticed his uneasiness and followed him. He lit a cigarette, walking slowly towards the car. She caught up to him and asked him, "What's wrong American boy?"

"I am feeling uneasy Nellie." Nick replied.

"Wait, I just have the right thing to get you to relax. You are just too tense, cousin." She took out a rolled-up joint of marijuana.

They got into the car, and parked it on the darker side of the entrance, playing some dim music, pushing back their seats and opening the sun roof.

They started smoking in silence, as they were both unsure how the other felt about smoking reefer. Nick broke the silence with a question, "*Have you ever been in love?*" Nellie laughed out loud looking out the window. The question made her shy. *"You are a weird guy. Where is this coming from?"* She asked, defending herself. *"Just curiosity,"* Nick replied. Nellie paused as she puffed away her worries, blowing her smoke as if she was in slow-motion. *"I don't think I have ever".* Nellie added. *"What about Frits? Don't you love him?"* Nick asked, perplexed. She giggled again, passing the blunt to Nick and blowing more smoke, her eyes diming down. The weed was kicking in. *"Are you serious with these questions?"* Nellie asked. *"Yeah, I actually am."* Nick replied trying not to laugh. He was getting high as well. She let out a little burp from the beer she had been drinking. "Sorry!" she exclaimed, placing her hand in front of her mouth. She laughed again. It was getting hard for her to control her laughter now. "I have never been asked these questions so bluntly. You have really become westernized. An American boy," Nellie laughed again. "With that kind of reaction, I think you have answered the question," Nick added. "I don't really know. At times, I feel like it can happen to me. It happens to others. What about you Nick? American boy, have you ever been in love?" Nellie asked. "Once. It was a while ago. Her name was Fatima, but I was more naïve then," Nick answered, staring at the stars. "The meaning changes when you grow up, I guess," Nellie added, feeling his hurt. "You talk like you have some experience in that department, though," Nick commented as they both laughed. "I think I was in love with my first boyfriend, but I must have been about seventeen or eighteen years old, and just needed to fit in. We had just arrived in Brussels, you know. Looking back, though, I think I was."

"What did it feel like?" Nick probed.

"Well, very happy and a sense of fulfillment. Just being together felt like I was on top of the world," Nellie answered, smiling and bobbing her head to the soft music that was playing. "Are you looking for this feeling again? You know, out of fear of weeping later, some people don't accept the joy that is knocking at their doorstep," Nick added. "Yes, I got hurt bad. But it is a great feeling indeed," Nellie answered, almost falling asleep. "What music do you listen to? I believe that music expresses that which cannot be put into words and that which cannot be silent."

"Wow, that is deep. I listen to all genres, but mainly ragga. It just makes me want to dance. I enjoy it most when I dance it with someone else. It's got so much rhythm and base. Love it." Nellie replied mimicking some dance moves.

Nick started singing *Till my baby comes home* by Luther Vandross: 'Don't you remember you told me you loved me, baby/ You said you would come back this way, babe/ Baby…baby…baby, oh baby/ I love you/ I really do.' His singing made Nellie smile.

"What do you think about before you fall asleep?" Nellie asked.

"What if this? What if that? I'm curious," Nick answered. "Yeah, me too. I think about the future and things that would make me happier," Nellie added.

"Happier? Aren't you happy? You are married to a very nice and responsible guy. You have Stephane. You told me that he is doing well at school and he is healthy. You have a beautiful house. Why are you not happy?" Nick asked with a tone of sincere surprise. "I am comfortable but not happy." She answered back. "Ok! Fair enough. What's lacking then?" Nick asked. "Nice question" - Nellie paused. "Something is missing. I feel like…"

A knock on the window interrupted her. Two policemen with rifles were patrolling the area and wanted to be sure that they were not having any intercourse in their car. They were on the lookout for such things, as it was an avenue for bribery.

Nick and Nellie were ordered to get out of the car. They got frisked violently. While Nick remained calm, Nellie was erratic. She spoke in Kirundi and argued frantically with them. She gave them a wad of cash, after which they disappeared without thinking twice. The cousins then entered the restaurant in a hurry, distraught. She told Chantal what had just happened and told her that they had to leave. She did not feel safe anymore, so she started persuading the others to leave the place. She particularly wanted one of the guys named Eloge to follow them, as she had a particular interest in him.

Eloge was a few years younger and had spent the last decade in the French-speaking part of Canada as a political refugee. However, he was tough mentally and an entrepreneur. He sold second-hand and refurbished cell phones from Canada to various African countries. He was his own boss. He had a deep voice. He spent a lot of time in the gym in pursuit of a body shape that he knew women liked in men. He basically had a big mouth, in the sense that he always spoke his mind regardless of how it made the other person feel. Some would deem him to be an alpha male. Inevitably, Nellie got attracted.

They all left in a cortege, going to one of the only night clubs open at the time. It was safer if they stuck together, because there were army road blocks all over the city that were there to ensure that people did not violate the national curfew; another avenue for bribery. They gathered at a night club called Archipel. On their arrival, everyone was already drunk. The motley crew was super excited, all emotions glaring, each individual with his own agenda but outwardly adhering to the group dynamic.

Nick had lost touch with reality due to the

marijuana. Nellie was becoming uncontrollable as she kept on downing gin and tonics. Nick all of a sudden started feeling paranoid. *What would Michel think of me if he saw me right now?* Nick asked himself. *My kid brothers died and I survived. Now look at me. Is this the best way to honor their death? I do not deserve this life. Mom should have lived. She was just the kindest. She deserved the education, the book publishing, the good food and wine I ate in Paris. God why did you have to take mom?*

He put his hand in his pocket just to check that he still had his wallet and identification. They were there. He felt a wave of relief. The disc jockey started playing a popular song from the US. Nick felt consoled by the familiarity of the tune and the effect it had on the people present in the club.

Without realizing it, he began dancing all by himself. He gesticulated like a buffoon in the middle of the dance floor, trying his best to mimic the dance moves from the kids back in the US at the time. They called the dance the *Harlem Shake*. Nellie was flirting with Eloge when she noticed Nick letting go of himself dancing like a nitwit, and she couldn't help but feel relieved to finally see vulnerability out of her cousin. Nobody ever has everything figured out. Seeing her cousin in that state, she grabbed Eloge's hand and led him seductively to the dance floor. They starting dancing, syncing their hips in a sexual motion. She didn't care anymore; all she wanted was to do what she was not supposed to do. Eloge thought that he had everything under control. The rest of the group, including Chantal, formed a circle, as each person of the group entered the circle and started balling out in ecstasy, encouraged by chants and whistles by the group of friends. Nellie moved away from Eloge and joined in the circle. She started dancing as if she was possessed, moving slowly in tune with the beat and touching herself in a sexual manner. The motion of her hips hypnotized all the men who watched her. Her hands touched her private parts, moving up to her breasts and ending with one finger in her mouth as if she was an innocent child who did not know how naughty she was – a mixture of innocence and sexual aura. She was just captivating. As the song changed, she left the circle to get yet another gin and tonic. At the bar, she met people she knew. They hugged and screamed with joy. They took shots of tequila, reacting as if they were disgusted by the poison they had just ingested in their fragile bodies, but they liked how it made them feel: free from their worries, responsibilities, their mistakes and the daily life they had chosen to live. They just wanted to be who they really were inside.

It was 6am and the sun was rising. The DJ was playing his last song. Nick was exhausted physically, mentally and emotionally. He asked Nellie if they could go home. Nellie had become aggressive. She did not want to leave. Nick tried to put some sense into her head but she was out of her mind. Eloge was walking past them when she just grabbed him and kissed him in front of everyone. She then pushed him away and told him that she was married and started laughing. Chantal grabbed her hand and they both disappeared in the ladies' room. Chantal came back out and told Nick that he would have to take a cab because Nellie was not ready to leave quite yet. She gave directions to the cab driver and sent Nick back to the house.

*

Frits opened the door for Nick. He looked extremely annoyed. Nick felt extremely ashamed. He told Frits what had happened. Frits calmed down and told him that they would talk when he woke up. Nick struggled to go up the stairs, swaying and lurching with every movement as Frits watched him fail to walk up the tiny flight of stairs. "I hope you are proud of yourself now, counselor?" Frits commented in a rather sarcastic tone.

Nick, unable to pay attention to what Frits was saying, reached his room, where he collapsed and blacked out instantly. Later in the day, Nick got woken up by the unbearable heat. His head pounding, he felt awful.

"I will never drink again. For sure this is the last time," Nick whispered.

He was feeling hungry. He slowly walked down the stairs, drowsy, with bad breath and reddish eyes. He looked sick. He saw Frits in the living room reading Nick's novel while his son Stephane was watching TV. Frits ordered his son to go play outside. They then sat in silence for a few minutes or so as Nick gulped ounces of water.

"I bet you are thirsty," Frits commented

"I feel awful. You cannot imagine," Nick replied

"I can imagine. I tried this lifestyle for a brief period in my youth. Drugs, alcohol and sex. Fortunately I quickly realized it was detrimental to a person's karma." Frits said.

"What do you mean karma?" Nick asked perplexed.

"I mean the sum of somebody's good and bad actions in one of their lives." Frits replied.

"Are you talking about reincarnation?" Nick asked, confounded.

"I believe that our actions have so much power that it not only affects our own lives, but those around us, our loved ones, our children and our children's children. Whether we like it or not, we live through them and them through us." Nick remained silent as he pondered at what Frits was saying.

"Are you planning to go out drinking your whole time while you're here? Is this what you envisioned yourself doing when you planned your trip coming back here?" Frits asked with a tone of disappointment. "I guess I needed to get it out of my system. I needed some form of release therapy. Me being here has drained me of all my self-control strength. I am swayed by all kinds of emotions that I did not imagine that I could feel. I am giving myself a break. Plus, all this is making Nellie happy," Nick replied. "That is how most alcoholics start, by giving themselves a break." Frits answered, while focusing on Nick's book. "Where is Nellie anyway?"

"You tell me," Frits answered rather sarcastically yet again.

"I left her at the night club." Nick exclaimed.

"She came home a few hours ago. She is fast asleep in the second guest room. I could barely recognize her. Now she is going to be asleep the entire day. Even our son Stephane has been asking me why Mommy sleeps so much lately. Do you imagine that?"

"Does she always drink this much or is it just the festive mood?" Nick asked.

"This behavior is new to all of us. She had a miscarriage last year. We lost our second child. Before Stephane was born she had managed to get a good job at BNP Pariba. She was a star in fiscal economics but had to take a break in order to take care of our son. She never found the strength or motivation to go back to it. I see her with our friends' kids. It is never the same with Stephane. Maybe he is a constant reminder of what could have been. I don't know exactly what it is, but it has been getting worse over the last decade. The frustrating part of all this is that we never get to talk about it. All I'm sure of is that the miscarriage was the tipping point." Frits answered. "Who's idea was it to come back to Burundi?" Nick asked. "It was actually mine. I figured it would help us to change our environment due to the miscarriage. We led a hectic life in Brussels. I worked a lot, but made a lot of money. She hated the cold and never got along with my friends or acquaintances. I managed to get beside myself and realized that we could have been heading in a disastrous direction. I proposed the idea of a getaway to her. It pleased her. So here we are. Now I have to deal with Chantal and the rest and I do not like the way things are turning out." Frits answered candidly. "Have you really tried talking to her? As in what do you guys talk about intimately?" Nick asked. "That is a very interesting question Nick. I will have to get back at you on that one," Frits answered with an air of surprise.

Frits noticed how Nick was suffering from his hangover. He stood up without saying a word and fetched two aspirins out of his medicine box. "Take these and eat something. It will help you feel better," he said, then threw Nick's novel in front of him and added, "You have a lot to offer to people around you. I urge you to make this trip meaningful."

Nick remained silent as he resisted reacting to the avalanche of emotions that clouded his thoughts. Those words reminded him of Michel. It reminded him how much he wished he had father around to teach him how to be a man. Guys like Frits or Michel were wise, but they were not his father. He wanted it from his father.

Later in the day, Nick woke up as the sun was setting. He went to check if his cousin was still asleep. There she was, snoring, her arms and legs spread wide like a star. He did not know how to feel; he just accepted what he saw. The hangover was fading, as he was getting back to his senses. He could not find Frits or Stephane. It was a Saturday, and so he decided to go get a sense of what normal Burundians did on the weekend.

He hopped on a *taxi-moto* and headed for the lake shore. He got dropped at a very popular beach next to the port. Most common Burundians hunged out there, those that spoke Swahili more than Kirundi. They tended not to have cars, did not go to fancy schools, and did not hold fancy managerial positions nor official functions. They got drunk on the cheapest beers and got pleased and entertained by the simplest of things. They were full of dreams but almost gave up on them as they had no idea on how they could surmount all the numerous obstacles they faced. So they drank, danced to music and experimented with various drugs. They basically indulged in activities that soothed their feelings of inferiority and sadness. Nick needed to understand this particular feeling of inferiority and how it affected an individual's life, because he did not know how to deal with his.

He wore beige shorts, a black polo shirt and a, NY baseball cap worn backwards. He wore his reading glasses as he was going to read *Animal Farm* by George Orwell. As he started walking in the sand, he saw a group of people that had gathered. He sensed chaos in the atmosphere. He heard screams and people arguing. Drawn to the brawl and low mumbles, he got into the spectating crowd. He found a half-naked woman holding a large beer bottle, drunk out of her mind, venting her frustration to the crowd about how she lost her husband to two fishermen who usually fished with him. She lamented on how one fateful day the three of them went on a fishing trip together as they always did. At the end of that day, only two of them came back. Her husband was missing. At that particular time, there was a shortage of fish and fishermen did not manage to reach their normal quotas; anxiety was rampant as their catch basically meant their livelihood. She accused them of having thrown him into the lake. She explained how they did so as a form of sacrifice to whatever creature or mermaid God ruled the deep waters in order to appease it so that it could release the flow of fish. It sounded absurd, and Nick could not believe what he was hearing. She further explained how she had never been the same since. She searched, and went to the police, but all to no avail. She went to see pastors, gurus and witch doctors to get justice, but nothing worked. Frustrated, she started drinking to alleviate her trauma. It destroyed her. It annihilated her energy. It confused her, making her hallucinate.

Nick walked away after hearing enough as he perched under a palm tree to ponder on what he had just witnessed. The events he had just witnessed made think about HAPPINESS. He wondered what made it so fleeting; he did not even know what it meant. Was it love? Was it the ability to love? Was it the sensation of being loved unconditionally? Could it be security? Peace? What about the stillness of the mind. He got stuck on the idea of HOPE and how it could be the precursor of it. Why does the grass always seem to be greener on the other side of the fence? He reasoned that everybody is in love and irrationally attached to the concept of *"what could be"*. That is the essence of the wealth of a youthful mind – having options, having the ability to dream. Reality is probably just too boring; slow or unengaging. That little fantasy of ours; that little secret is the only thing that keeps us going. Some people call it hope, others view it as goals, and spiritual souls call it faith and the professionals, vision.

However, Nick found it odd how happiness was always in the future - never in the present.

These philosophical thoughts got interrupted by an old bum playing beautiful music on a dingy homemade guitar. The music was hypnotizing and soothing, but let out feelings of despair, hurt and disappointment. The small waves smashing on the reef mixed with the complex guitar riffs made it sound like a symphony of life - a life of sadness counterbalanced with a consoling promise of hope. It quickly got dark and Nick headed back home.

*

As he arrived back at the house, he saw Frits in his car arguing with Nellie. She was standing on the front porch yelling at her husband. Frits put the car into reverse and dashed out of the compound, almost running Nick over. Nick took a deep breath and approached the main house. He followed Nellie inside the living room.

"Is everything alright?" Nick asked.

"I can't take this anymore, I just can't," Nellie kept mumbling to herself, walking around aimlessly like a headless chicken.

She was dressed quite provocatively, with a tight and extremely short black skirt. She had lots of make-up on, making her look like she was out looking for trouble. Her perfume filled the room as she grabbed some keys, her cell phone and her purse. Nick asked her if she was going out. She did not answer. She walked towards the door and looked back. She smiled, batting her luscious eyelashes and said, "I wish he could understand."

She received a phone call. She picked it up, answering in monosyllables. She then told Nick that Chantal was waiting for her, and disappeared into the darkness, struggling to walk in her high heels.

Nick, filled with ambivalent feelings, went up the stairs and heard Stephane giggling as if he was with someone else. He entered the room and found an undone bed as if someone had just jumped out of it. He noticed one of Stephane's little toes protruding from underneath his bed. Nick got down and asked the boy what he was up to, and the kid told him that he was with '*Bernada*' and '*Bolida*', his imaginary friends. Nick asked him why they had such odd names. The boy answered that they had unique names because they were special. He was sure that nobody else in the world had the same names as his imaginary friends. They were his secret. They were loyal only to him. They protected him and always told him that everything was going to be OK. He trusted them because they never let him down, never left him alone and always did what they promised they would do.

Nick returned to his room and laid down on his bed, his hands folded behind his head. He started pondering what Nellie and her husband were going through. He concluded that gluttony was an inordinate desire to consume more than one required. We usually think of a glutton as someone who indulges excessively in eating or drinking. The chief error about gluttony is to think it only pertains to food and drink. Even though gluttony does mean eating or drinking too much, it nevertheless denotes far more than that. Gluttony is an emotional escape, a sign that something is eating us. It has to do with need. A need that is unfulfilled and frustrated for a long period, that is thwarted again and again, will seek outlets. Such an outlet, among many other possibilities, may be gluttony. Overeating and drunkenness are symptoms of a larger problem of over-indulgence, lack of self-control, boredom or anxiety. When someone falls into the temptation of gluttony, he or she does not only want to eat or drink without limits but devour the whole universe, assimilating and possessing everything exterior, reducing the surroundings to oneself. Physical appetites are an analogy of our inability to control ourselves. If we are unable to control our eating and drinking habits, we are probably also unable to control other habits such as those of the mind (lust, covetousness, anger). This also means that we are unable to keep our mouth from gossip or strife - the inability to say "no". However, possessing the ability to say "no" to anything in excess is one of the fruits of the spirit. Excessive enjoyment through the senses will result in the senses enjoying you.

*

Nick later went back to Gitega and visited Kibimba, the notorious place where the atrocious slaughter happened. It has since become a place of reconciliation. It has been commemorated by converting the old petrol station where it happened into a monument with the legend, *'Plus jamais'* (never again!) inscribed on it.

AMOS

- THE BEST FRIEND -

CHAPTER TEN

The car fumes were suffocating Nick as he rolled up the window. There were lots of cars, but none were moving. "Is this normal?" he asked Amos.

"Welcome to Nairobi, boss!" Amos replied jokingly. Nick was shocked to see traffic jams as bad as those of New York City in an African country like Kenya. "People are making money here, you know. Things are happening in this region. If I were you, I would seriously consider settling here," Amos said. "You don't say, huh!" Nick replied rhetorically.

Nick and Amos's families were neighbors back in the 80s in Gitega. They spent a lot of time together as kids and went to school together. They were best friends. In 1989, Amos's father found a good job as a project manager for the UNDP in Nairobi, relocating his family to Kenya. They kept in touch from time to time, but as their respective circumstances changed gradually, so did their friendship. Amos's family planned to come back to their native country as their contract was about to expire, but the war broke out. Amos's father renegotiated a contract and stayed in Nairobi to avoid any harmful conflicts. They stayed out in Kenya for the whole period of the war until it calmed down in 1997. Amos's mother had already established herself as a successful businesswoman as she opened up a successful restaurant and later a bakery in Nairobi. His father contracted HIV from one of the numerous other women he squired, and without knowing it passed it on to his wife. The sickness really affected Amos's farther psychologically. He gave up on life, seeing himself as a failure. He passed away in 1999, leaving behind a terminally ill widow and three children. Amos had an older sister and a younger one. He had to become the man of the house. He rose up to the challenge, but he had one problem that prevented him from becoming the person he really was: he loved women. Nevertheless, he had a brilliant mind.

He was easy on the eyes, with a great smile and an aura of likability. He inspired trust and intelligence. He was eloquent. He could talk to anyone from any social class. He seemed to know everyone and everyone knew him. He was the go-to guy. However, no one understood him, so he understood everyone else in order to suppress the frustration of not being understood. He was a frighteningly good judge of character.

*

They drove up to his apartment, unloaded Nick's bags, and perched on the balcony of his third-floor flat. Amos offered him a beer to unwind and break the ice. Nick gracefully declined. There was no awkward moment of silence as Amos had the knack for the art of conversation. He had great general knowledge, followed international news, read a lot, and rarely criticized, condemned or complained. He gave honest and sincere appreciation and always managed to arouse in other people an eager want. He smiled a lot, and never forgot how important it was to remember a person's name. He made it a habit to carefully listen when people spoke, without interrupting, and quickly followed with well-thought-out and relevant remarks or comments.

They chatted and reminisced on good old times, talked about what they were up to during their time apart and all the events that led up to this reunion. Nick quietly and nonchalantly described how he lost his loved ones, meeting Michel and Sigourney, living in New York, graduating with honors, publishing his book, going to Paris and returning to Kibimba. He explained how he was starting to feel more at ease with himself the more he confronted his fears. Amos hinted at his disappointment in his father. He actually pitied him and blamed him for some of his own setbacks, but mainly his mother's sadness. Amos adored his mother.

During his college years, Amos met an exchange student from America called Maurice, better known as Reace, who he got along very well on many levels. They were both avid bodybuilders and athletes, and also both wanted to become big business moguls. After graduating, they managed to start their own business. They opened up a gym on one side of a road and a pharmacy on the other, which sold common drugs and supplements. Amos would take care of the administrative side, while Reace managed the products and services. Reace was a serious bodybuilder with lots of energy, while Amos was a smart and extremely ambitious chemist.

Amos had a modest demeanor, and was always dressed smartly. His hair was always neat, and he listened a lot and kept his earnest comments and thoughts to himself when in public. He was a true Burundian. Reace, on the other hand, was the complete opposite: he was the epitome of a modern young "Black American", who embodied the hip-hop culture and frustration. He spoke using a lot of slang, dressed quite unorthodoxly for the Kenyan community, and exuded such confidence that it bordered on bluff or phoniness. He was very muscular, and had some exquisite tattoos all over his arms: his two daughters on his left arm and a Bible verse on the other - 1

Corinthians 13.

"If I speak in the tongues of men or of angels, but do not have love, I am only a resounding gong or a clanging cymbal. If I have the gift of prophecy and can fathom all mysteries and all knowledge, and if I have faith that can move mountains, but do not have love, I am nothing. If I give all I possess to the poor and give over my body to hardship that I may boast, but do not have love, I gain nothing. Love is patient; love is kind. It does not envy; it does not boast. It is not proud. It does not dishonor others; it is not self-seeking. It is not easily angered; it keeps no record of wrongs. Love does not delight in evil but rejoices with the truth. It always protects, always trusts, always hopes, and always perseveres."

Their common interest as friends was books and the goal to attain the most knowledge one could acquire. They loved understanding how things worked, whether the issue was a practical, social, political or philosophical one. Amos was inspired by Kwame Nkrumah and Nelson Mandela, while Reace quoted Malcolm X and Marcus Garvey. They debated and amicably argued mainly on pan-Africanist views and beliefs, but they always got sidetracked by their passionate relationships with the opposite sex. Most women were attracted to them, each in their own way. They both had an uncanny relationship with women that could be traced back to their childhood and upbringing. The interesting part was that no matter how different their personalities, childhoods or upbringing were, the result was always the same. Sex!

Growing up, Amos was always surrounded by women. He got in tune with what they liked, what they were scared of and what motivated them – he basically understood how they viewed the world. He learned a lot from his sisters and their friends. He learned about life from his mother and what a man is supposed to do from her friends. But sex? He got that from the house maid, Mary.

He must have been eleven or twelve years old back in the mid-1980s when they still lived in Gitega. Back then he was a normal boy who hated doing homework, loved playing soccer and enjoyed Chinese kung fu movies. In school he kept overhearing the older boys talking about this thing called sex and *"blue movies"*. Bear in mind, back then sex was still taboo, and censorship was still rampant. There was no internet! Nevertheless, he never really understood what it meant. His male peers also discussed and rated girls in their class and were intrigued and wondered what they had to do to be liked in order to have this thing called sex. He never really thought too much about it, as he was busy collecting mangoes so that he could sell them. Even at his young age he knew how important and liberating money was.

One normal day, Amos and his Arab friend Salim were going around town looking for unattended mango trees collecting as many fruits they could during their free afternoon after school. They decided that they had collected enough and would return at Amos's house to separate the good fruit from the bad or small ones. Even at that age they already had a knack for business and an unconscious understanding of competitive advantage. At the back of the house next to the servants' quarter, where they could not be seen by anyone, they would organize and or count their money. Lo and behold, just on that particular day as they were counting money, Amos sexuality got ignited.

He noticed the house help, Mary, through the window, butt-naked fresh out of the shower. She was drying herself slowly with a thin pink towel, which she then threw onto her thin, small bed. She picked up a bottle of body lotion and started jerking it up and down so that the cream could flow easily. She then opened it and let it come out so gently into her tiny hand. She placed the bottle on the table and started applying the cream ever so slowly, gently and sensually all over her petite body. The sight of her massaging herself with the cream was hypnotizing. The two boys had never seen a naked woman before. The way Mary applied the lotion to her body almost seemed as if it was a performance. She would lift one leg on the bed and start from her feet ever so meticulously, up to her thigh, caressing her left butt cheek and looking at her beautiful brown skin with pride. She would do the same ever so calmly with her right. The boys were frozen. They just stared in silent amazement, their mouths open. Each had forgotten about the other. They felt weird and were feeling something very powerful happening in their crotches. Their breathing was fast, and they kept wondering what would happen if they were caught. It was an amazing moment, and they ignored any possible repercussions. Just at that moment, Salim started opening his trousers as the bulge in his crotch became uncomfortable. He let his manhood out, and felt free. He felt as if it was natural for him to massage it to soothe his discomfort. Just as he did so, Mary caught a glimpse of the little voyeurs at the window and screamed out loud like in the movies, covering her breasts and sex. "What are you doing there? I will tell your mother."

They panicked, all the while laughing mischievously. Salim, under the pressure and fear of the moment, caught his manhood in his zip and squalled like a tiny piglet. In the heat of all the action, Amos tried to help his friend by freeing his manhood, which was bloodied. Amos suggested it would be best if they called for help. Salim ordered him not to, saying, "My father will kill me if he finds out."

They ran away together, and went about their business. Amos returned home at about six in the evening and caught Mary's eyes as she was setting the table for supper. He was petrified but looked at her like she had nothing else to offer. All she could say was "you, you, you", nodding her head as if there was something she could do, but they both knew that she had oddly liked being seen. He acted like he didn't feel anything and went straight to his room and lay on his bed. He smiled. Right there and then, he understood that all a woman wants is to be desired. His new quest now was to find out what the hell a "blue movie" was.

*

Amos was already on his third Tusker Malt when Reace came into the apartment accompanied by two luscious-looking ladies. The women joined the best friends on the veranda. Everybody got acquainted and exchanged many politically-correct, kind words. The two ladies were Christine, Amos's official girlfriend, and Amanda, Reace's fiancée. They were very attractive girls, with desirable curves, and well spoken. It looked like the housemates and business partners had everything under control: their own apartment, their own business and loyal girlfriends. After a while, Amos decided that it would be best for Nick to meet his mother and sisters because Nick was only around for a few days before he went back to his job in New York. He reckoned that it would be hard for them to find time to meet again.

They got into his Honda, which smelled of leather and featured an exquisite music system. He listened to R&B and soul music. The vibe was very cool, calm and seductive.

"I bet the girls get really comfy in your car," Nick joked.

"The more relaxed the target, the easier it is to bend them to your will." Amos replied jokingly the beers having an effect on him.

"You devilish charmer," Nick added with a sadistic laugh.

"Well, you know, funnily enough, people are narcissists. They are drawn to those most similar to themselves. If you seem to share their values and tastes, to understand their spirit, they will fall under your spell." Amos said.

He was about to elaborate more on his understanding of charm and seduction when he rolled down his window to give some very mundane and banal instructions to the compound security guard. As they drove out, there was another traffic jam after only a few meters. This time, apparently, the country's President was on his way to the airport and his security had stopped traffic for a little while as his Excellency and his sixteen Mercedes -Benz cortege followed protocol. "Wow, there are some things that I will never understand. The whole world has to stop just because of one person. As in one person is going to the airport. Did you know that the prime minister of Singapore only has one car, one police bike in front and one at the back for security? Fifty years ago Singapore was as poor and underdeveloped as Kenya. The tiny country of four million people is now amongst the richest, peaceful, cleanest, least corrupt countries in the world. And their prime minister only has one car." Nick lamented. "Well, the secret to capturing people's attention, while lowering their power of reason is to strike at the thing they have the least control over: their ego, their vanity and self-esteem. You will not seduce anyone by simply depending on your engaging personality or by occasionally doing something noble or alluring. Seduction is a process that occurs over time. The longer you take and the slower you go, the deeper you will penetrate into the mind of your victim. What you are after as a seducer is the ability to move people in the direction you want them to go. We are creatures who cannot stand feeling that we are obeying someone else's will. Should your targets catch on, sooner or later they will turn against you. But what if you can make them do what you want them to without their realizing it? What if they think they are in control?" Amos commented. "Wow, I would have never thought that you were entangled in these manipulative power games." Nick added. "Well Nick that is how life is. This is the game you have to play to survive and get what you want. What I'm telling you is the pure reality of things. Tell me that throughout your life so far you haven't found yourself having to persuade people – to seduce them? It's OK, you don't have to answer. I don't want to make you uncomfortable."

*

They arrived at Amos's mother's house. By the size of the gate, it was evident that she had made something out of herself regardless of her sickness. There were many dogs howling and barking as they entered. There was a pool and a big, well-tended luscious green garden. Interesting to see how people evolve Nick thought to himself. I guess the grass is greener on the other side of the fence.

As they entered the house, Amos's sisters jumped up to greet Nick with fervor. They were accompanied by their husbands and children. Amos's mother was the most dramatic, hugging Nick tightly, almost in tears. She looked oddly healthy for someone who was HIV-positive. She grabbed his head in her arms and said, "Look at you all grown up."

She hugged him as if she had found a lost son. She knew what had happened in Kibimba and understood all too well the pain of losing a loved one. She grabbed his hand and started introducing him to her daughters' husbands and kids.

CHAPTER ELEVEN

Amos's mother, sisters, brothers in law, nephews and nieces and Nick, were all eating the desert after devouring a well prepared meal as Amos' mother talked about her late husband. She told them how much of a smooth talker he was, full of life and ambition. He always wore a hat slanted on the side with a cigarette at the side of his mouth. He wanted to be like Frank Sinatra. He loved partying and being around people. He fed off people's energy and loved charming everyone he met. Innuendo was his trick. You never saw him coming. He was attractive - a major player of the game of life and seduction.

All her words and the look in her eyes as she spoke so rapturously about him made Amos very uneasy. His heart was pounding. He kept calm, but could not control his face. He hated it when somebody was venerated for exploits that were so undeserving of respect or praise. He wished she would tell of the nights when she would wait for him until dawn, not know his whereabouts, and he'd come back either drunk, or smelling of women's perfume and lipstick on his shirt. *"I'm meeting some colleagues,"* or *"I'm going to work late today"* were his favorite excuses. If that did not work, or got old and overused, he altered it to "I'm working on a deadline" or the best - "I will be back in an hour."

Amos wished his mother could tell them about when his dad got caught red-handed by the maid with his wife's niece, or the maid herself, or the neighbor's maid, or the scandal with the Swedish intern. Or about the most hurtful betrayal: with his wife's best friend. He wished he could tell them of how the man beat him, his sisters and mother when he got angry or when they did something he deemed wrong according to his standards. Amos's father did not discriminate, and loved himself and the rush philandering gave him, weather it was with a maid or high-class businesswoman. It must have been have been too good for him to think ahead to the consequences.

Amos had had enough, and started up a conversation that took everyone by surprise.

"Well, Nick, is it true that you have written and published a book?" he asked out lout, totally changing the subject.

Nick took his time to answer the question as he had told Amos everything about his book earlier. He looked at his friend, wondering where all this was going. He answered, "Well, yes, I published it last year. I wrote about the minorities in the different corners of the world and how inferiority complexes paralyzes people, and I paradoxically elaborate on how the people who manage to overcome these complexes achieve extremely great things.," Nick answered in a very monotonous tone. Everyone at the table politely expressed their amazement, and Amos added, "That is very inspiring, Nick, especially from a black man, better yet as a Burundian. I actually finished reading Things Fall Apart by Chinua Achebe. Do you know he is the only African author who has won the Nobel Prize for literature? I am sure that gives you lots of motivation?"

"You may say so," Nick answered, still confounded about where Amos was going with these comments and questions.

"Well I find it inspiring. In the book Achebe talks about how polytheism and polygamy are the custom in their community. He beautifully describes and talks about the rule of men and the role of each member of the family. The men are overly domineering. The women and children are treated poorly and often beaten. Life in Achebe's Nigeria of the 1890s just before the British Colonialism would seem very different to someone living in our modern days, wouldn't you say that?" Amos asked with a sadistic smirk on his face, looking at his mother.

    The room went awkwardly and painfully silent. Amos's older sister and kindest at heart offered more dessert. Her husband accepted the offer, trying to loosen up the tension. Amos's mother's smile got wiped off her face. She looked at Amos with a menacing look, then smiled again nervously, hiding her shock at this betrayal by her son. She then calmly defended herself. "My children, let me share a secret with you. I promise you will thank me later. What women really want is to be thrown up against a wall by a man who is powerful enough to do it, yet gentle enough not to hurt you in the process. Well, at least not a lot. Our biology as women is in direct conflict with our psychology as women in modern society." Amos's older sister joined in the conversation in support of her mother. "I totally agree. My boss, a high-powered TV producer, compared her current boyfriend, a white-collar bank executive who thinks of her as her equal, and her previous boyfriend an uneducated cyber-café owner who thought of her as her woman. Verdict? Well, sex was way better with the cyber café-owner, because he had no problem shoving her up against the wall. The bank executive well, a milquetoast in bed but a good provider. I think all these dynamics are confusing. So I totally agree with Mom."

As the evening went on, they talked and debated on

very interesting and current issues. They went into a long discussion about love, throwing around words like *passion* or *infatuation* and *lovesickness*. Nevertheless, they all agreed on the fact that culture has a profound impact on people's perceptions, experiences and feelings about love, and about what is permissible and appropriate in their expression of love, romantic love and passionate feelings. The interesting part was that the women at the dining table were the most verbal. This intrigued Nick.

While everyone was yapping and expressing their own opinions, Nick kept thinking about how women's role in society had changed and how the women's movement may have been the most momentous social upheaval in our lifetimes. Though its origins lay in Euro-America, it was rapidly spreading around the world. On the flip side, a Greek philosopher once defined man as a rational animal. If you think about it, you will realize that this is a terrible definition. Man may be a thinking animal, but much of what men do - maybe even most of what they do - is neither logical nor rational. Euripides was far closer to the truth when he described men as full of conflicts, irrational desires, and as creatures that were very hard to understand, especially in regard to their treatment of women.

*

As the evening came to an end, they were all standing in the parking alleyway. Amos and Nick were about to leave when Amos's mother thanked Nick for having taken the time to visit. It meant a lot to her, and she made sure he knew that he was always welcome. Nick reciprocated by thanking her for being hospitable, cheerful and hopeful despite all the negative events and circumstances in her life. It was a definite sign of strength on her part, and he told her that she inspired him. His words really pleased her. She asked him jokingly, "When are you getting married?", to which he replied "the day Amos does." Everybody laughed. It was the last time Nick ever saw Amos's mother, as she passed away a year later.

*

The boys headed to town to catch one last drink before calling it a day as it was the middle of a busy week for Amos. They were going to meet up with Reace. The ride through the city center was a quite one. Maybe they were each processing the things that were said and done during the dinner, or maybe Amos was remorseful for humiliating his mother. Why do men humiliate the women they love? *Maybe I am just like my farther*, Amos thought to himself.

Nick kept observing the buildings, surroundings, and billboards, the people, the street lights, the awful public transportation, the air of barely contained violence, the dirty streets, the prostitutes, the bad drivers. He paid attention to everything.

Arriving at their destination, the parking lots were all full. One street kid freed a reserved parking spot for Amos, who must have been a frequent customer. The bar was called '*Florida 2000*'. It looked fairly sharp, but its seediness soon showed itself. It wasn't the classiest of bars, but one of the most popular. It was one of the best nightclubs in Nairobi at the time, mainly due to its novelty for Kenyans. There you could find girls doing lap dances, table dances and for something small or bigger you could get a girl there for an hour or more. Within three minutes of entering, the local girls descended on them aggressively with a questionable motive: prostitution, also known as the oldest profession in the world.

At the bar, Nick could see some British tourists, also with a questionable motive, trying to pick up some of the local women. Women sell; men buy.

Next to the dance floor were some female Japanese tourists bouncing back and forth between being quite and demure and screaming and tearing up the dance floor. As they walked across the dance floor, they spotted Reace in the lounge with two buddies of his, surrounded by three "working" women. Everyone looked high on some form of drug or alcohol. One really big and luscious lady was table dancing with razzmatazz, braless, with her D-cup breasts jiggling and her over-sized gluteus maximus shaking. She wore a tiny black thong, enticing the men watching her. Reace was smoking marijuana, watching the woman with explicit frolic and malice in his eyes. Desire: sex was on his mind. In fact, sex was on everybody's mind. The most salient fact about sex is that nearly everybody is interested in it. Most people like to have sex, and they talk about it, hear about it and think about it. But some people are obsessed with sex and willing to have sex with anyone or anything.

A few hours ago they had just met his fiancée, and now he was there openly philandering with hookers and strumpets. Reace was from the ghettos of Los Angeles, where there was a rampant inferiority complex like any other minority community in other parts of the world. His essence consisted of gaining power and being significant. Reace viewed power as the willingness and ability to kill, control, manipulate, oppress, humiliate and torture other human beings. The only way he knew how to be significant was through private power – the most dangerous form of power. In this sense, sex became an expression of malignant private power and also represented intimate reprieve from the rampant struggle between private powers in the public realm.

As the best friends walked toward Reace, Nick whispered to Amos that he did not want to stay in such a place. Amos looked at him, smiled, and told them that they would not be staying long. They approached Reace's table and greeted him. Reace had changed his demeanor. He was arrogant, full of himself and high. Amos decided to go to the bar and have a drink there with Nick. "Don't take it personally. That's just Reace. He is in his zone," Amos commented, ordering a small beer. "So is this where you guys hang out?" Nick asked, sipping on his soda. "This is Reace's spot. Personally I am not into paying for it," Amos replied. "What about his fiancée?" Nick asked again. "How can you stay faithful in a room full of hoes? You ask too many questions, Nick. Sometimes it's wiser to read between the lines," Amos replied with a fake laugh.

As they posed at the bar, women kept on pinching Nick's behind or softly elbowing him, all the while giving soft seductive winks. Nick couldn't help but stare, intrigued at these girls' bold advances. He was just not used to this kind of environment. Generally, gender experiences have a great deal of influence on sexual desire. As a boy enters adolescence, he hears jokes about boys' uncontainable desire. Girls are told the same thing, and told that their job is to resist. Now Nick found himself in a situation where this whole dynamic was reversed. It was madness.

Looking at what was happening in the nightclub, it would seem as if the scientists were right: men, like other animals, are simply striving to survive and to reproduce. Thus what they want is as much sex as possible with as many women as possible. But Nick still naively believed that deep down all men did not want unlimited promiscuous sex but something rather different. What men really want is to win the love of a princess or a girl who deserves to be a princess, to fight against great obstacles, to deliver her from dragons or a wicked witch of a stepmother or some other great danger, to deliver her and to live happily ever after.

"My turn to ask you questions," Amos commented in a joking manner. "Do you have a girlfriend, Nick?" Amos added. "I do not." Nick answered. Amos looked at him, perplexed, straining his eyes. He unconsciously did that whenever he was in deep thought.

"Have you ever had a girlfriend?"

"Once, but it was really a longtime ago. I was just a teenager," Nick replied.

"Are you still a virgin, Nick?" Amos asked in a mocking tone.

"Yes."

"Yes? You are trying to con me, right? Come on, tell me the truth. You're still a virgin? Really?" Amos asked, confounded again.

"I'm not trying to hide my hairy palms, but I haven't told this to anyone yet. I am planning to become a priest. A real priest. A man of God."

Amos froze with the beer in his hand. A long stare…

"What?" Amos exclaimed.

"Hahaha" Nick laughed.

A fight broke out in one corner of the club. Two working girls were fighting over an American tourist. As they got bored watching two drunk prostitutes fighting, the best friends looked at each other and laughed. That's when they decided to leave the club. Nick stepped out on to the street as if he had come out of a filthy dirty place, scraping at himself as if he was dusty. He put his hand inside his pocket and reached for his cigarette pack, then patted himself, looking for his lighter. *Shoot, I gave it to one of prostitutes who asked for a light,* Nick told himself. Funny how, lighting a cigarette for a woman is a non-verbal pick-up line.

As he looked around, trying to find a lighter from someone, he noticed a homeless bum. The hobo looked confused and a bit bonkers. Although the guy was talking to himself, pointing fingers and all, he looked happy and secure in his madness. Did he choose his circumstance? Was this his destiny? His purpose? Just as Nick observed him, a fair-skinned, thick-thighed woman in high heels and with long, fake hair walked right past him, mincing her derriere daintily. She paused and adjusted one of her shoes, bending over and sticking her apple bottom right in the hobo's face. Right there and then, for just a minute, he became sane. He smiled and pointed his finger towards her.

The little scene made Nick laugh. He then thought of how sex was a desire with no equal. *What really happened with the snake, Eve and Adam?* Nick thought. *How good did that forbidden fruit really look or taste? Was it worth it?* The apple in the Garden of Eden looked deeply inviting, but you were not supposed to eat of it. It was forbidden, but that was precisely why you'd think of it day and night. You see it, but cannot have it. And the only way to get rid of this temptation is to yield and taste the fruit.

Amos was done talking to people outside the club. They hopped in the car and started driving slowly around town. They bought some egg sandwiches in a dingy place on the streets. For some reason, food always tasted great at 4am. They drove around listening to some old-school rhythm and blues, talking about their dreams, goals and plans and exchanging funny stories. They were re-bonding. Amos got a bit more sincere and candid, as a light touch and humor always disarmed and opened people up. He was seduced by

Nick's easiness and calmness. "Were you serious about the whole becoming a priest story?" Amos asked. "Well, the more I grow up, the more I realize how much I know nothing. As each year passes, I feel empty. Nothing seems to do it for me anymore. When I was young, just for a brief moment, I felt whole. Needing less but yet feeling like I had everything I ever needed and wanted." Nick answered. "Wow, that must have felt like heaven." Amos added. Nick laughed sarcastically and added, "Funny how people use that phrase. Like heaven! How do you know how heaven feels like? Surely not like an orgasm! If that's the case, then I'm missing out on God…HAHAHAH!" He laughed pensively.

A brief moment of silence…

"Do you want to know how heaven feels like to me?" Amos asked with a child-like tone. "Yeah, sure, why not? Tell me what God feels like," Nick replied with intrigue. "I used to love live band music. I used to get a kick going to church because they had a live band. They played every week. I must have been eleven or twelve years old and I could not go to bars or events that played live music on my own. So the church band was my only way - my muse. I just loved the sync all the band members had. Imagine, the drummer, bass, keys, the bongos and the guitar. They all played different sounds, had different rhythms and notes. Individually they sounded amazing, but together they sounded whole; fulfilling. It just sounded right."

"Wow, that's poetic." Nick said jokingly.

"One day at a fair, the church band had a stand and was about to play all day long. While they were setting up, the drummer was putting his drum set together, when I approached him. I told him how much I loved the drums the most out of all the instruments. I loved the whole idea about it. I told him how much I wished I could learn how to play. I told him that I admired how well he could play. The constant beat that always had a snare and kick, always hitting at the right and same time. I asked him if I could try. He was probably on a tight schedule. He could have brushed me off or nicely told me that he didn't want anyone to tinker with his set. Instead, he told me that I could do the hi-hats and snare, while he would do the kick with his foot. I told him that it was hard and that I couldn't do it. The tricky part about the drums is that you have to use your whole body playing different rhythms at the same time. In order to play well, your right hand had to be as good as your left, while kicking with your foot. I managed to get the snare and hi-hat right while trusting the drummer to hit the kick on cue. To my surprise, it sounded right. My older sister, who was in the choir, watched me and cheered for me. Then everyone around stopped what they were doing or saying and started watching us. They started clapping and cheering for us. I felt like I was on top of the world. We stopped and I looked at the drummer. He was smiling and clapping as well. He acted as if I was the one doing it on my own, giving me all the credit. He told me, "Well young man, you see that you can do it.""

"What's your point?" Nick asked. "Our only purpose here on earth is to achieve perfect union with God." Amos answered.

A Nina Simone song was playing in the background as they drove slowly in silence the rest of the way back home.

CHAPTER TWELVE

That night, Nick could not find any sleep. He kept thinking about what Amos said: *"Our only purpose here on earth is to achieve perfect union with God."*

When he did finally manage to close his eyes, he had weird dreams: colorful images of odd pictures and drawings that he saw on Jehovah's witness leaflets when he was a kid, where lions and sheep sat together in perfect harmony, kids played with an elderly couple, or a group of people had a picnic in an ever GREEN loan, sharing fruits and cupcakes. There was a black kid, an older Caucasian man with a thick moustache, a Chinese woman and an Indian adolescent looking happy, without any worries, all enjoying each others' company.

*

Nick opened his eyes and checked his watch, spilling a cup of water that sat next to it in the process. He sat up, let out a low grunt and placed his head in his hands. He got a flashing image of one particular hooker who looked just like his deeply hidden fantasy girl. He tried not to think too much about it. He looked for his cigarettes, but the box was empty. All of a sudden he wanted a cigarette more than ever, or maybe it was the prostitute who had ignited his fantasy? He got up on his feet ever slowly. He was going to try his luck, looking for a fag in the living room. It was dark, lit only by a side lamp in the corner of the living room. He looked on the coffee table – nothing. He looked in various drawers, and still could not find anything. Went into the kitchen and noticed the trash can. He thought about it, and still all he could think of was at least one puff. So he went digging in, looking for a cigarette butt. He didn't care if it had been in the trash for hours; all he wanted was one smoke, a puff to ease the itch. As he rummaged through the trash, a cute girl caught him. She was also fetching something from the fridge wearing only wearing Amos's shirt. She had a tiny piercing in her nose, wore mascara on and had beautifully braided hair. She was not completely African, nor completely Caucasian. The mixture of heritage and genes made her a breathtaking beauty, with black curves, polished and symmetrical facial features, and a hint of green in her eyes.

"Hey!" she exclaimed in a sexy, husky voice.

"Hey!" Nick exclaimed in a deep rock voice.

She smiled; he smiled back. She looked like a girl Nick knew from before, but it wasn't her. He wished it was her.

"Do you have a cigarette, by any chance?" Nick asked. "Yeah, I was about to have one. The only one, though. We can share it. I'm Bella, by the way, and I am not going to ask you why your hands are in the trash can." Bella smiled.

"I'm Nick."

"I presume you're Amos's friend from America?" Bella asked.

"I'm actually from Burundi, just like him. But I live there."

"Wow, must be nice living there?" she said as she lit the cigarette. Nick looked with desire at the way she lit the cigarette and put it in her mouth. He admired the shape of her lips as she inhaled and imagined the feeling of inhaling the smoke, soothing his itch. He wasn't sure what he wanted more, the cigarette or

Bella.

"Where are you from?" Nick asked trying to make some conversation.

"I would say Kenya. My father was Kenyan; my mother was Greek. They passed away a decade ago."

"Sorry to hear that. My parents passed away a while ago too. So I'm sure I know exactly how you feel. What happened to them?"

"Ah, it's a long sad story. Politics. They got assassinated."

"Ah, I know a thing or two about politics and assassination too."

"I don't want to talk about death today. I think we have suffered enough. Wouldn't you say so?"

"I think you are right." Nick replied, finishing the cigarette.

"Aren't you going to ask me what I'm doing here?" Bella asked.

"Well, yeah actually. I was wondering. I presume you are Amos's girlfriend?"

Bella burst out laughing…

"Sshhh!" Nick exclaimed putting one finger in front of his lips. "People are sleeping!"

"Who cares?" Bella exclaimed. "I am not his girlfriend. Don't play dumb, Nick. I'm sure you've met Christine."

Nick remained silent…

"It's OK dude. I know I'm Amos's side chick, but I'm OK with it. I don't feel sorry for myself. I know how real life is comparing to most people."

"What do you mean?" Nick asked. "I don't waste time fooling myself. I keep it real with myself. I know how men are. I actually feel sorry for Christine. She is naïve, but I don't blame her. Society has softened everyone with trumped-up ideologies by the greatest seducers of our time." Bella added.

"Let me guess. You are about to tell me that love doesn't exist." Nick commented. "Well, it does, but only one kind. The one a mother has for her baby, even if that baby is unhealthy or deformed. She will accept and love it the way it is. That is the only love I believe in. The rest is bullshit."

"So how would you describe your relationship with Amos?" Nick asked. "He makes me feel good just the way I want it. He is also honest about not being honest. He does not sulk if I do not call him back and never tries to impress me. But what I enjoy the most is that he feels at ease, natural or his true self with me. He tells me things that he can't tell Christine. Because Amos and Christine are fooling themselves." Bella answered. "Do you think that most couples are fooling themselves?" Nick asked. "Yes." Bella answered bluntly.

Amos came out, looking drowsy. He called Bella to come back to bed. The look on her face when she saw him gave it all away; Amos owned her. Nick later learned that Bella had been molested by her aunt's husband after her parents' death. The way she explained it to Amos was quite peculiar but interesting nonetheless. After her parents' death, she and her older sister had to go live at her aunt's house. Their aunt's husband farmed chicken in their backyard for their eggs and sold them. It was intriguing for the girls at first. They would help here and there as the chicken amused them. They got really excited when a new batch of tiny little chicks came in. They found them cute. As the chicks grew, it came time to cut their beaks. Bella wanted to have a go at it. As she approached the chicks, the birds would run away from her and gather in one corner squeaking loudly. But when her uncle came in, the chicks would squeak less and not run away, even though they knew that something bad would happen to them. They were ambivalent about their situation because of the familiarity they had with the uncle. She said that she was just like those little chicks.

*

Nick returned to his room and thought about passion. He concluded that lust is having a self-absorbed desire for an object, person, or experience. When we are in lust, we place the object of our desire above all things in our lives. It is often manifests itself as a self-destructive drive for some pleasure regardless of its value, merit, or legality.

The term usually stands for excessive passion for sexual pleasure, but it is any kind of passionate desire, whether or not it has to do with sexuality, which is indulged in a spirit of egocentricity or isolation. It is the childish attitude of "*I want to have*", without a true spirit of mutuality. It is easy to be deceived, because the stronger this selfish need is, the more the person may sacrifice, submit, and be a martyr. All this is an unconscious manipulation in order to get one's own way. Since this tendency is subtle and hidden, and often has nothing to do with sexual passions, it may not be obvious that it is lust. Yet all human beings have some of it. Where there is a forcing current and a driving need, there is lust.

We all have that, and it is even stronger when it is not yet consciously experienced. You may deceive yourself because that which you so strenuously desire may in itself be something constructive, yet you are the craving, needy child who wants to be the center of the universe. The raging need, which you may or may not be conscious of, is disconnected from the causes that brought about the original unfulfilled. In your ignorance, the need or lust swells to unbearable proportions and you become more frustrated because you do not see the remedy, which is a change of inner direction. In other words, an unfulfilled need that remains unrecognized in its primary, original form produces lust.

When a need is unconscious, a displacement occurs and a replacement need is pursued lustfully. No matter how legitimate, constructive, or rational it may be in itself, such a pursuit indicates immaturity. The stronger the urgency, the greater the frustration must be. It does not matter whether this refers to sexual desire, or the lust for power, for money, for being liked, or for a particular thing. When these emotions are investigated and the original need found, you can begin to dissolve the lust. You can come to terms with the original need, but you never can with the replacement need.

Nevertheless, of all longings and desires, none is stronger than sex. To assume that the sexual urge per se is sinful lust is utter distortion. Sexuality is a natural, healthy instinct. If it matures properly, it combines with mutuality and leads to love and union. If it remains separate, it is lust, but it is no more evil than the lust for power, for money, for fame, for always being right or for anything else. Sex as desire has no equal. When sex controls the individual, instead of him controlling it, the degeneration of that individual is already an accomplished fact. Sex is a blade that cuts through the bone. If the desire is not controlled, sex will destroy you.

That night, Nick decided that he would take up a celibate life. He concluded that he could not reach enlightenment while harboring perverted thoughts. After the conscious and bold decision, he finally managed to sleep.

Opening his eyes later, he felt well rested and

rejuvenated, feeling lighter, sharper but mainly wiser: conscious. He then realized that he was on a plane on his way back to New York.

SLOANE DREXLER

– THE DREAMER –

CHAPTER THIRTEEN

It was a cold January morning. The end-of-year festivities had just ended. New York was still hurting from the terrorist attacks on the Twin Towers a few months earlier. The sky was grey and overcast. Snowflakes had fallen all night long. They had brought with them frost, bitterness and melancholy.

Sloane got up after hitting the snooze button for the fourth time. Dread of the morning gave her a sad and drowsy look. She felt despair even before the day had started, tears and surrender before the first battle of war. These questions followed in her mind: *Why is life so hard? Why did I choose this job? Maybe I should have taken veterinarian courses? Maybe I should've opened a book store? Maybe I should have married Anthony, I would have been happier. It's too late now.* The hustle to change would be too tiring for Sloane.

She picked up the empty tube of Aqua fresh toothpaste, squeezing it to its limit with effort and fervor only to garner a tiny drop. She started brushing her teeth with lackluster apathy. She looked out the window as she brushed her teeth and saw Cathy her stray cat curled up sleeping in a box in the fire escape stairwell. Cathy looked very comfortable. The weather was conducive for sleep. It was early in the morning. *Oh, I wish I was that cat, she thought to herself.*

She dreamed of meeting the love of her life: rich, handsome and intelligent. She dreamed of getting married in a white wedding dress, having two children and living in a lovely house not too far from a tea plantation with a sea view, waking up to the sound of waves crashing on the reef. Sloane was always hoping that one day, without warning her Prince Charming would arrive, sweep her off her feet and take her away with him so that they could conquer the world together. While she was waiting for her Prince Charming to appear, all she could do was dream.

Dreaming was very pleasant, as long as she was not forced to put her dreams into practice. That way, she could avoid all the risks, frustrations and difficulties. She tended to always blame other people, preferably her parents, the husband she did not have or the children she did not rear for her failure to realize her dreams. But what were her actual dreams?

*

The dark-haired woman's fantasies and goals gave her a false unrealistic sense of security. She was slothful and put off what she should have be doing for herself, her family, her friends and community. She tended to be idle and not accomplish what needed to be done. She was dreaming about it instead, because she loved being lazy.

Sloth is the avoidance of physical or spiritual work. It is the desire for ease, even at the expense of doing what should be done. The slothful person is unwilling to put forth the necessary effort to fulfill worldly obligations and achieve self-transformation and spiritual growth. The slothful person wastes life's precious opportunities for growth and service.

Sloane had not always been like this. In her childhood, the world seemed like an enchanted place. She was born in the late 1960s in San Francisco, to a Korean mother and a German father who met at a hippy infested rock concert. They fell in love and got married after nine months of courtship. After living the hippy life to the fullest for a few years, reality struck the young couple. Her father decided to get a job, but his credentials and reputation did not help him in his endeavor. So he decided to go at it on his own and went into the refrigeration business. Her mother, a stay-home mom, was an artist and drew cartoons for newspapers and television stations as a freelancer. They always told their daughter that she could do anything she wanted and be who ever she wanted to be. Their way of raising their child had a good effect on her, especially in Sloane's early childhood. Everything that Sloane encountered had intensity to it, and sparked feelings of wonder. Now, from her mature viewpoint, she saw this wonderment as naïve, a quaint quality she had outgrown with her sophistication and vast experience of the real world. Such words as *"enchantment"* or *"wonder"* caused her to snicker.

The adult world confronted her with new challenges that were not simply mental or intellectual. Her line of work was demanding; she was on her own and the stakes were higher. Her work was now more public and highly scrutinized. She might have had the most brilliant ideas and a mind capable of handling the greatest intellectual challenges, but she tumbled into emotional pitfalls. She started to judge herself abnormally, which ultimately meant that her self-esteem was low. She therefore tended to always want to please people and relied on the opinions of the public.

She really carried this need for approval over into everything she did. Throughout the years she had started gaining some weight. She abhorred physical exercise. She developed an inferiority complex, which formed when she realized that she was not at the level she wanted to be at. This feeling arose when she started believing that she was not at the same level as her peers and that she was totally unable to deal with issues like she used to. This kind of complex demonstrated a her fear of confrontation with problem's and the conviction that she was unable to solve a problem due to her lack of preparation for that problem. This invoked tension, caused limitation in her actions, and made her static during trials or to move backwards in difficult situations.

She was afraid of adventure and wished to have an easy life. She feared the harm that could come to her self-esteem. The expressions of this inferiority complex in some situations caused her to create excuses and to be anxious. When she felt shame, it was expressed through anger or depression.

As she dressed for work, she realized she was going to be late, as usual. She dashed out of her apartment in a rush, leaving it in a mess. She caught the subway just in the nick of time. She found a newspaper on the floor. She picked it up and kept it as it had started snowing again. *I will use it to cover myself*, she thought, but an article caught her eye. It was a children's fable of why chickens could not fly. It went like this:

Many years ago all the birds could fly.

They lived and did everything together.

Every morning, all the birds would wake up before dawn and sing together then they would all leave to go look for food.

This they would do the whole day and return in the evening at sunset to share what they had gathered. However, one bird was always missing in action: the hen.

The other birds were concerned. They raised the issue with King Eagle. Complaints flowed in about how Hen would not join the others in their daily activities but she would be the first to wash her hands when it was time to eat.

One evening all the birds gathered in the palace as agreed. Hen was summoned and asked to explain why she wasn't participating in the gathering of food. She explained that she was always falling sick and had no energy to join others in looking for food. Besides, I don't get full when we share the little food! she added arrogantly.

The other birds were shocked at her response as no one talked to the king that way and got away with it. King Eagle immediately declared that Hen and her whole family were banished from the kingdom. Owl, the magician, was ordered to take back the flying powers from Hen and her family.

Hen left the kingdom with nowhere to go. She sought refuge in Man's land where Man soon discovered that he could make a delicacy out of her and her entire family. From that day, Hen can no longer fly and is eaten by Man more frequently than any other bird.

The little fable made her smile. She folded the newspaper and put her headphones on, and started mentally preparing for work. She worked as a dentist's assistant for a high-class reconstructive surgeon dentist who rented expensive office space in one of Marcus Hammond's buildings in Manhattan. Hammond & Weisberg Capital also rented two entire floors in the same building. The world-renowned Canadian psychiatrist *Dr Pierre-Claver* (a personal and good friend of Marcus Hammond) also rented prime office space in the same building. He headed all the four counselors that worked at Hammond & Weisberg in a special cousinage deal with his prestigious practice. Those four counselors included Nick, who happened to go to work early on that Friday morning as he was full of energy coming back from his fulfilling trip to Europe and Africa.

It was about 7:55 am when Nick stood on the marbled ground floor of the majestic building, looking fresh, healthy and sharp in his dark blue suit and tie. He was unaware of Luis Fernandez's presence, as Nick did not pay too much attention to baseball. Luis Fernandez was a former star MVP for the New York Yankees who happened to be going up the building. He had recently been involved in a catastrophic car crash the previous year, which put him in a coma for four days and ended the life of his girlfriend. They had allegedly been arguing the whole ride, and he lost sight of the road for a split second, hurling his Aston Martin into a tumble. There was a rumor that he had actually been pronounced dead until he came back to life after forty-five minutes. The tragedy garnered a lot media attention. He was probably in the buildings to seek counsel from Dr Pierre Claver.

Ashton Brolin was a small man, no more than five feet five, in jeans, reefer coat and a cowboy hat that made a clinging noise with his cowboy boots. He stood right next to Nick as the indicator of the elevator edged down ever slowly from the tenth floor. It froze at the first floor. The middle-aged cowboy was thin and gaunt, with deep wrinkles in the back of his neck. The brown blotches of the benign skin cancer caused by the sun of the Texan oil fields were on his cheeks. They ran down the sides of his face, and his hands had the deep-creased scars of handling heavy machinery. None of these scars were fresh; they were as old as erosions in an oil-less desert. The reason was that two years earlier, Ashton - now better known as Mr Brolin had hit the jackpot at the state lottery in his little southern Texan town. Eighteen million dollars was the figure. Ashton needed the up elevator as well, probably going to get some wise counsel on how to manage this new enormous amount of money sent from the Gods above at Hammond & Weisberg.

As the elevator doors opened up, the three men entered the elevator. Nick asked which floor they were going to, as he had designated himself as the button pusher. As the door started closing, a large, hairy black hand came in between the two sliding doors, halting the process. The tall black man whore a grey uniform with his name written on his chest: 'Ekiti'. He held the two doors as if he was waiting for someone. Sloane entered the elevator in a rush, exhaling a breath of relief and avoiding all eye contact. Ekiti entered as well, feeling good about himself for being so chivalrous. The five souls were all headed up, each in search of their own quests yet in the same vessel. The lift ride from the ground floor to the sixteenth was quite normal until it suddenly halted and got stuck between the seventeenth and eighteenth floor. Everyone remained silent, as nobody could really fathom what was actually happening. They all looked at each other, slightly perplexed. The elevator had jammed in between floors.

After another brief moment of silence, Nick panicked and started pressing buttons, trying not to show his anxiety. He tried the button to open the doors, but it did not work. "*Ummm, I think this thing has jammed!*" Nick exclaimed in a high-pitched voice as he started pushing the alarm button.

The fact that there were other people there made the ordeal less frightening for Nick. He pressed the alarm button one more time, and Ekiti tried as well, pushing Nick out of the way, but to no avail. Ekiti asked who had a phone handy so that they could call the police. Ashton wagged his head from side to side without opening his mouth. Nick removed his cell phone from his pocket and noticed that the battery was almost dead.

Luis removed his phone and called the police. The person at the receiving end said they would send help immediately. Nick called the building reception and asked for help. He got the same calm answer from the receptionist as the police dispatcher. He hung up; checked his phone: only four percent battery life remaining. "What do we do now?" Nick asked. Ashton finally opened his mouth, saying, "We patiently wait".

CHAPTER FOURTEEN

They all stood there for a moment in stunned silence. They all secretly thought the exact same thing: *this cannot be happening.* "*Elevators don't get stuck in real life!*" Sloane exclaimed.

Nobody answered apart from Ekiti, who smiled. After a few more minutes of staring at each other and waiting for something to happen, Nick finally realized that they were not going to go anywhere unless they did something - but what? Who knew the protocol for being stuck in an elevator? "*What are we going to do?*" Luis the baseball player asked. Sloane sat down on the floor, her reflection in the mirror starting to get on her nerves. "*I wonder if anyone is even around.*" Nick asked rhetorically, sitting down as well, and leaning his head against the wall. Mr Brolin seemed to be calm about the whole situation. His breathing and demeanor were slow and braced.

Mr Brolin wanted nothing more than to be one of the guys in rural South Texas where he was raised. Two years had elapsed since he had the misfortune to acquire almost nine million dollars from the state lottery. Today he had lost his anonymity, his buddies, the girlfriend he'd once had and most of his family whom, he no longer trusted. He rarely ventured outside the trailer where he lived alone, and the four dogs he kept chained outside were his only companions.

Oddly enough, he wished he had not won the jackpot. His attitude towards the money had startled most in his Atascosa County farming town of four thousand souls not too far from San Antonio. Ashton had been an average guy before he won the eighteen million jackpot, greeting each day with a purpose: to eke out a living as a drilling rig "floor hand" in the oil and gas fields where he had worked since he was in his early twenties. He'd been part of a community of laborers, no different from anyone else. Today, with no need to earn an income and no set routine, he had little to occupy his days.

*

Suddenly Ekiti said, "Hey, listen. I think I hear someone coming!" Sure enough, someone was coming down in the other elevator. *"Ring the alarm! Ring the alarm!"* Ekiti yelled. Nick punched the button and held it down. They all stood in silence, listening and waiting for something to happen. Nothing. As the other elevator neared theirs, they could hear people talking as if nothing had happened. *"Are they just going to ignore us?"* Ekiti exclaimed, with a twinge of hurt and betrayal in his voice.

Ekiti was a Cameroonian student turned immigrant, who had come to the US to pursue serious studies in international relations, as his father (a staunch Muslim faith practitioner), worked as a high-ranked and well respected UNHCR coordinator in various African countries. However, Ekiti lost his way and briefly forgot his values after his first year at Columbia University, indulging in excessive partying and pursuing a career in hip-hop music. He played around with girls and knocked a girl from Barbados one night when he was drunk. He got faced with reality when she refused to have an abortion. His family got the news and shut him off, mainly because of their beliefs and what such a situation would do to their reputation. It really hurt him, and he lost any motivation he had, getting depressed for a period of three months. Fortunately enough, he picked himself up and decided to become more responsible, especially for his unborn baby. His strategy was an intriguing one: he decided to quit smoking cigarettes. Yes, bizarre, but this was his thought process. Deep down, he adamantly believed and understood that an addicted mind plays tricks on itself because the addicted mind pushes negative feelings to the back of itself. Ekiti really found refuge in cigarettes, and believed that they were his friends, but he never really felt anything positive in smoking. He simply felt weak, trapped, guilty, ashamed, and controlled. His willpower was never sufficient, which increased these negative feelings. He truly believed that all the things he did and the ways he felt were indeed caused by his addiction to nicotine. That goes for any other addiction that one might use to soothe negative feelings. He thought that by quitting he would inevitably either reduce or quit alcohol. If he managed to contain the alcohol, then he wouldn't have an urge for the clubs and bars where most of the binge drinking took place. If he managed to contain the nights out, he would have fewer chances of frequenting odd women or have malicious motives. This in turn would force him to focus on something more fruitful than feeding his ego, so he decided to start his own business. He used the remaining four thousand dollars he had and created a cleaning company. He cleaned many different floors in the building. His work was in such demand that he had no choice but to hire two other employees. Things were looking better, except that now he was stuck in an elevator.

*

It went quite again. Luis Fernandez sat down, sliding down the wall as if he had gotten shot. Ekiti took a seat out of despair, with a worried look on his face. Mr Brolin was the only one standing, still looking unmoved, serious and silent, until he opened his mouth for a second time, *"Are the stories of you dying and coming back to life true?"* Everybody turned their heads towards Luis, waiting for a candid answer. "I mean, we might not make it out alive today. You might as well tell us what happened," Mr. Brolin added. "I don't think anyone can understand," Luis Fernandez responded. "Try me. I work with Dr Pierre-Claver. I know a thing or two about understanding people." Nick joined in the conversation. "You're a shrink? Aren't you young to be a shrink? Sloane snickered. Nick just looked at her and cracked a cold smile. "What about you, miss, do you have a career, or you are working towards one?" Nick replied. Sloane kept silent and lowered her eyes, avoiding contact. "It's OK, young lady. I have had basically the same job for almost twenty-five years of my life until I unfortunately won the lotto two years ago," Mr. Brolin added, trying to make Sloane feel good about herself. "What do you mean unfortunately winning the lottery? It's everybody's wild dream of winning a vast fortune of money without working and breaking your back for it. Isn't it?" Sloane enquiring. "Shoot, that's the 'truth-Ruth' right there. Ha Ha!" Ekiti joked while giving Sloane a high-five. "Well, things don't pan out the way you expect them to. Picture this: people now call me 'sir' or worse – 'the millionaire'. I hate going out because I don't want to run into people who owe me money, or people who want money. I'm arguably the richest guy in my small town – everyone always wants something. Distant relatives and the fair-weather friends keep coming clamoring for their share.

Kidnapping and murder suddenly became very real threats. But the greatest danger to myself is myself. People who are in the same situation as me either lose the money or themselves or both."

"In what way?" Nick asked.

"Geez, shrink. You love questions," Sloane commented.

"I was convicted last month for assaulting a bar manager. Two casinos are suing me for allegedly bouncing checks in excess of $500,000. You know, for a moment I considered myself fortunate. I spent years praying I'd win the lottery. I envisioned a leisurely life for myself in a nice house, surrounded by family, in the county where I was raised. Suddenly everyone wanted something, so I bought a car for my parents and several cheaper ones for my friends. I loaned out a few thousand dollars there, a few thousand dollars here – my memory is a bit faulty now. I can't tell you who I exactly lent money to, but all I know is that no one ever pays me back. I started treating money like it was a renewable resource. I didn't manage to ditch my trailer though." Mr Brolin continued his story.

"Do you miss your old job, or are you finally pursuing your dream job?" Nick asked.

"I don't miss the oil field, but I am not searching for a new one either. For now I just shut myself away in a trailer, discourage visitors and take a swig of beer by 4pm. If I need food, I pay someone to get it for me. How do you like the lottery now, kids?" Mr Brolin answered bitterly.

Nick kept quiet and thought to himself, deducing from what he had just heard that time was of the essence. We are temporally limited creatures. We live. We die. In the time in between, we are called to be our "true selves". This may be considered to be in the likeness of God, whatever that may mean to you – life is short. Time is precious. To waste and squander it through sloth, laziness, procrastination, task avoidance, lack of motivation, desultory or dilatory behavior is a sin against life itself. Sloth represents the pseudo-solution of withdrawal from living and loving. Where there is apathy, there is rejection of life. Where there is indifference there is laziness of the heart that cannot feel and understand others – and cannot, therefore, relate to them. Nothing produces more waste than sloth, apathy, and withdrawal. A person who has a positive, constructive attitude toward life will not be slothful. Someone who is not preoccupied with personal safety will not withdraw, and therefore will not become apathetic. Sloth always indicates selfishness. If you are too afraid for yourself, you will not risk going forward and reaching out toward others. Whoever reaches out takes the risk of being hurt and accepts this risk as worthwhile.

*

Mr Brolin finally sat down. He looked relieved. Everybody had a consoling demeanor towards him. Another uncomfortable moment of silence prompted Nick to speak out, "How bad was that car crash, man?"

"They said, well, he is in heaven now. I could hear them speak the words, but I could not feel myself." Luis Fernandez answered.

"Wow. So you briefly died, right?" Ekiti asked in a child-like tone. "After a few minutes of total darkness, I felt all my senses, but I was in a place that looked desolate. I was alone. Felt like I was in another country. There were no hills; it was just flat. It looked semi-arid, with little plants or no vegetation. I guess it looked like a desert. Then I saw the light." Luis Fernandez said. "Really, dude? You saw the light?" Sloane snickered.

"The light had taken me out of my body. I heard angelic voices and lost all feelings. The light was very comforting, warm and disarming. I trusted it. I wanted to speak to it, but my power speech was taken. The light told me that it had a lot to show me. As I looked out, I saw a place where a multitude of people gathered and their appearance was like that of the light. Their color was pure white and their bodies seemed to glow with radiance. These lights were looking at a bright light that shone like the sun. It was the source of all the light there. They were all looking at it as if they were seeing something there, but I could not look at it as they did. I heard the sound of many instruments and the sounds were like nothing I had encountered before. These lights were worshipping God with one voice and raised their hands as they were singing. I longed to join them, but the light stopped me. I will show you hell now. He called it outer darkness. The light raised his hand and as he brought it down, the gates ripped open with a great noise. I could hear the crying and wailing of many people, but the light did not allow me to see any of them. There were many people there, but unlike the souls in heaven, the appearance of these people there was as it had been on earth. They were from every race, culture and nationality. Every person seemed trapped in their own personal torment, a torment that would go for eternity, and they could not communicate with others. The sounds of the crying and wailing were almost deafening. I did not see any flames or demons, but I could feel evil. I could feel the gritty sand-like substance under my feet. It was horrible. Even if there is no flames the people I saw there had no hope, no second chances. They were lost forever and eternally separated from God. Suddenly, they all seemed aware of me and started crying to me for help. But they only called out to me, as if they could not see the light next to me. The light then told me that this place was not meant for any human being created by God. It was not meant for human beings; he made that place for the devil and his agents. But the stubborn human beings who will disobey God, like the devil, will also go there." Luis Fernandez paused for a minute, a tear falling down from his right eye. Trying to hide his face, he put his head in his hands and wept, saying, "God sometimes gives us visions about the future to warn us. The light then told me if the book of my life was to be closed today, this would be my portion: hell. I told him that I went to church every Sunday and did my best to do good. The light told me that on my way to the hospital I asked God for forgiveness, but could not forgive my girlfriend, so my sins have not been forgiven. It is a matter of reaping what one sows. I cannot sow unforgiveness to my girlfriend and reap forgiveness from God."

Right there and then, they all heard a muffled voice calling out, "My name is Mike, I am here to rescue you. Are you guys all right in there?" They all jumped to their feet as Ekiti shouted, "Hey, Mike, help us. We're stuck in the elevator. It's not funny at all."

Everybody got rescued without any physical harm, and all things got back to normal faster than expected. Everybody went their separate ways acting as if this event had not somehow changed them. The truth was that it had a profound effect on all of them, especially Nick and Sloane.

Nick went straight to his office, where all colleagues welcomed him with open arms, as they were all worried for his wellbeing. He explained briefly what had happened until the people lost interest. Finishing his social duties, he went to his office and lay down on the psychiatrist's couch, exhaling his anxiety. He calmed down and relaxed. He could still not believe that he was stuck in an elevator for ninety minutes with four other souls. It was kind of a wake-up call for him, and he felt that the other four souls felt the same thing. The event made him think about 'action'.

Acting now is in our best interest. We know this - nothing is stopping us from acting - but we still somewhat irrationally delay our actions. We all have the tendency to want to take the quickest, easiest path to our goals, but we generally manage to control our impatience. We understand the superior value of getting what we want through hard work. For some people, however, the inveterate lazy streak is far too powerful. Discouraged by the thought that it might take months or years to get somewhere, they are constantly on the lookout for shortcuts. Their laziness will assume many insidious forms, and if you are not careful and talk too much, they will steal your best ideas and make them their own, saving themselves all of the mental effort that went into conceiving them. They will swoop in during the middle of your project and put their name on it, gaining partial credit for your work. They will engage you in a "collaboration" in which you do the bulk of the hard work but they share equally in the rewards. His thought processes got interrupted by a phone call. He jumped to his feet and answered it with class and professionalism. It was his supervisor, Dr Pierre Claver.

"Nickolas? How are you? Is everything alright?" Pierre Claver asked in his thick French accent. "Yes, sir. I'm fine, thank you. It was actually enlightening," Nick replied nonchalantly.

"Ah! Interesting. We will talk about it later in the day. I also want you to know that the big boss wants to see you."

"He wants to see me? OK. Should I be worried?"

"Actually, he does not want anybody else to know

about it. He wants you to meet him at 6am tomorrow morning at his penthouse."

"Is this a joke, sir?"

"Do I sound as if I'm joking? You cannot say no by the way. It's actually an order."

"If you say so. Do you know what he wants?"

"He just wants to talk."

"OK, I will be there."

"Very well, young man."

He hung up the phone and wondered what Marcus Hammond, the man with the Midas touch, could want from him.

"What a day this is turning out to be!" Nick whispered.

He felt like taking some air. He put his jacket back on and decided to take the long flight of stairs down. He was on the twenty-second floor. Without thinking too much about it, he started going down the stairs until he reached the nineteenth floor, where he noticed Sloane in her ubiquitous white vest uniform puffing a smoke in the stairwell.

"What a crazy day this is tuning out to be, huh?" Nick noticed her sad eyes and decided to sit next to her and said, saying,

"You bet."

"Do you smoke?" Sloane asked. "Yeah, why not. It will help me think straight." Nick answered. She took a cigarette out of her purse and gave it to Nick. Nick could already feel the bonding. This looked all too familiar: having a puff with a girl he had barely met. Maybe it's easier to talk to people who don't really know you, Nick thought.

"Do you know what Ekiti told me after our rescue? He told me that by dropping his smoking habit he managed to garner enough will and inner strength to quit all the other nasty habits. He told me that everything is linked and that the smallest of actions create the biggest results," Sloane spoke after a minute of silence. "That sounds deep. Do you have nasty habits that you want to get rid of?" Nick asked. "You are a shrink for real, huh?" Sloane asked jokingly. "I'm an objective listener. But a shrink nonetheless." Nick answered. "Well, I don't know how to define my state. I think I'm depressed. However, the issue is that I never thought I could be depressed. I always think of these tough periods as just tough times. But nowadays it has become impossible. It's really hard for me to get out of bed in the morning. I just want to hide under the covers and not talk to anyone. I don't feel much like eating and now have lost a lot of weight." Sloane explained. "Isn't that a good thing? Losing weight?" Nick probed. "Well, I have lost it in an unhealthy way. Nothing seems fun anymore. I am tired all the time and don't sleep well at night. But I have to keep going because I'm taking care of my little sister, and although I have a decent job, it's unengaging. If feels so impossible, like nothing is going to change or get better."

Nick inhaled from the cigarette as she smoked, looking very pensive with a very assuring calm demeanor.

"Well, deducing from what you just told me, I can guarantee that what you are going through is a classic description of depression. However, you are not alone. It is quite common especially among women. May I ask how old are you?"

"Twenty-eight. Why do you ask?" Sloane answered.

"*Just like that.* Did you know that this depression of yours can be effectively treated?"

"Dude, I don't need a doctor. I just need a break."

"Ok, Ok, I get it. Tell me more about your little sister."

Sloane paused and smiled as she thought about her

sister. From the look on her face, her little sister brought a lot of joy in her life. "She is a good girl." Sloane said. "I think that you will find yourself, your voice and meaning to your life by taking care of her," Nick commented as he stood up. He looked at his watch. "Listen here, lady, I got to run. I presume you work in the building. Ask for Nick up on the twenty-second and we can continue talking. Take care." Nick said. "I'm Sloane, by the way, and I will definitely pass by." Sloane replied.

Nick immediately ran down the stairs until he reached the ground floor. He went to the nearest Starbucks coffee shop and bought a latte. It was cold and grey outside. He put some earphones in and played his favorite Nina Simone song, *Nobody Knows When You're Down and Out'*. It made him think about laziness and depression. When you are slothful, you do not give a chance to life, to yourself, or to others. Such life negation cannot ever be resolved unless you come to see this basic selfishness and self-concern as unhealthy. Sloth is one of the defense mechanisms in your fear of being hurt: you defend yourself by becoming lazy and indifferent towards everything that is life-producing. This particular sin necessarily begins with the assumption of agency, or free will. We are free to choose, and it is on the basis of this choice that we are open to praise or blame. Sloth begets blame - the ultimate blame in fact. We work for praise and to avoid blame. We struggle with weakness of will. We seek forgiveness in our own way, and try again.

At the very least, sloth is a hindrance or obstacle in life. In addition, blame is cast on the slothful individual. Sloth is a vice because it contributes to the individual's failure to achieve his or her true self-expression.

As he finished his coffee, he stood outside, took out

one of his cigarettes and put it in his mouth. As he was about to light it he remembered the words Sloane told him about Ekiti and the whole ditching of the cigarettes. He lit it up anyway and went back to work.

MARCUS HAMMOND

-THE BOSS-

CHAPTER FIFTEEN

The modern, avant-garde digital alarm clock kept blinking: 4:27...4:27...4:27...4:28. The room was freezing cold. The veranda door was wide open. There he was, Marcus Hammond in the flesh, in his chinchilla fur coat, sitting by himself outside, in the middle of winter, with his third cigar in his left hand and a very expensive cognac in his right. His nose was red as a clown's as he watched New York's skyscrapers from his enviable Park Avenue penthouse. He felt as if he was coming down to his last days. The maverick was feeling like an old man now. He was lonely and unloved. Hurting and tired of living. He tended to be a bit melodramatic, and thought that he was ready for the hereafter, "*It has to be better than this*" he thought.

He once owned all the appropriate toys: the yachts and jets and blondes, the homes in Europe, farms in Argentina, an island in the Pacific, thoroughbreds, even a soccer team. But he had grown too old for toys. The money was the root of all his misery – opportunity cost.

In his youth he sacrificed what most people deemed important things and actually succeeded in his endeavor to attain perpetual riches. Nevertheless, he enjoyed it by himself. "*It's very lonely at the top,*" he would mumble every time he felt lonely, consoling himself.

For just one minute, he wanted to give it all back or exchange it for all the love and relationships he'd forgone for all the material wealth he'd acquired. For a minute he wanted to be like everyone else: having people around, sharing, and being connected in a deeper way. His first wife would call him empty and selfish. He would tell her that she had no personality and backbone, saying "That is why everyone walks over you." She would burst into tears every time he spoke those words, and he would just look at her crying, feeling victorious for having the last word. "Nothing is enough to the man for whom enough is too little," as Epicurus once said.

He grew up in an era and as part of a culture where people struggled to get to college and get a decent degree. During school, or very shortly thereafter, people got married and started having kids. Getting a job and working your ass off at it was considered the ticket to a good life. He followed this pattern without a lot of thought. He found work to be enormously exciting, and saw the weekends as a time to play golf and party with other young couples. But there he was, sitting all alone in the cold, clearly realizing that the balance he'd chosen had consequences for the people around him at home and at the office. For instance, his daughter Lucy was raised by her mother (his first wife), alone. In his early days on Wall Street, he used to show up at the office on Saturday mornings. Not coincidentally, his employees showed up too. He honestly thought that those weekend hours were a blast. They would mop up the workweek in a more relaxed way and shoot the breeze about sports. He never once asked anyone if there was someplace they would rather be, or needed to be – for their families, favorite hobby, or whatever. The idea just didn't dawn on him that anyone would want to be anywhere but at work. In the early 80s all his employees were all men. Many of those men were fathers, and fathers were different then. They did not, by and large, attend ballet recitals on Thursday afternoons or turn down job transfers because they didn't want to disrupt their kids' sports "careers".

Most of their wives did not have jobs with their own competing demands. In general, it was assumed that wives stayed at home to make everything run smoothly.

*

Marcus Hammond was born on August 26th 1945 in Newcastle, England. He was born on the exact same day as hundred thousand people attended the victory parade in their city, in order to celebrate and cheer for their troops. He was born in a time of relief, hope and victory, even though his farther was not around to see him take his first breath. His father, member of the 11th armored division, had died in a fierce battle in German-occupied Netherlands in March 1945. The war ended two months later. His mother never remarried, and things quickly returned to their sour taste.

Newcastle was a rough place to grow up in. His mother worked at a bar, and picked up a nasty smoking habit. Whisky and weary men followed. In their household, there were only two topics of conversation: politics and soccer. Working at a bar, she had no choice but to love the game. She brought up three children on her own on a North Kenton council estate. The two other boys were her nephews, who were also orphans by that time – deceased father and abandoned by their mother (her sister). Marcus considered them brothers, but the rivalry between them was evident from the start, mainly due to the fact that Marcus wasn't pampered anymore. Money was short, times were tough, meat was a luxury and their clothes were hand-me-downs. Everybody had to toughen up quickly or drown in the ever-rising tide of the harshness and reality of life.

Not much scared Marcus's mother, but he would never forget the look of fear in her eyes when she talked of debt. When she fell ill, she would worry that they would not be able to pay for her funeral. She in turn had grown up in the 30s, during the Depression. She had seen what debt could do to hard-working families on difficult times.

From such experiences of deprivation and lack, Marcus came to perceive life as being unreliable and limited, but containing a missing ingredient for happiness. "My well-being depends on me getting all that I desire. I cannot truly be myself a whole person until I get what has always been missing." He even went further in his train of thought, adopting a frighteningly self-centered doctrine: *life is limited. There isn't enough for everyone. I miss out because other people are taking my share, getting what is rightfully mine. Once I have it all, I will never lack anything ever again.*

He became gripped by this same fear his mother had: the fear of lack - the fear of having to go without something essential as there may not be enough of it to go around. He left his native city of Newcastle to try his luck in the Big Apple, looking for a better-paying job and a more eventful life. He ran away to New York to escape the role dictated by his background and conventional wisdom, but mainly to discover what he could do on his own. He wanted to see if he could make a difference in the world, that he was unique and valuable. He felt that he could not achieve that in his hometown. New York was the center of various events. He would be able to be in the middle of a melting pot of opportunities. The city was populated by black people, Arabs, Chinese people, Koreans and Indians. Diversity!

He lived and worked in Manhattan, the heart of NYC - It was the center of business, his trade. People were always in a hurry and where most important events took place there. By the final quarter of the twentieth century, the US had evolved into the most sophisticated system for generating investment capital the world had ever seen. America was creating wealth, they marveled, because America appreciated the wealthy. They had created a financial superstructure that enabled the wealthy to translate their fortunes into investment that enriched the lives of all Americans. Thanks to these marvelously efficient superstructures, any American with a business idea worth exploring could get a shot at success. America had created in a sense an entrepreneurial heaven on earth. The inevitable outcome of capitalism was that it rewarded greed and short-term gain and turned high-flying chief executive into celebrities.

Marcus had graduated from the University of Oxford with a BA in Mathematics and Statistics, financing most of his tuition by playing poker. He briefly worked at Riverbank House in London as a credit analyst. Unhappy with his position, he decided to get a business degree from the London School of Economics. While at LSE he met an American student called Carl Weisberg. Carl introduced him to the Asian and American markets. Marcus got hooked, but his gambling habits got him into some serious trouble with some serious people. He owed a lot of money; he had no choice but to runaway to the US.

CHAPTER SIXTEEN

It was still completely dark and freezing cold when Nick failed to open the main door. Nick rang the bell and looked at his watch; he was five minutes early. The man in the security uniform let go of his doughnut and buzzed him in. "You're Nick, right? Go up to the top floor. He is waiting for you," the security guard ordered.

As the elevator doors opened, Nick was still wary from the elevator incident the previous day. The doors opened across from the penthouse door. He saw three men in black walking towards him. The two on either side had shaven heads and faces that looked as if they had been carved none too expertly from granite. The man in the middle had hair – although not that much, and from the looks of it, it seemed as if each strand had been individually combed into place. The two shaven headed men folded their arms across their chests and stared unblinkingly at Nick. The man in the middle was dressed entirely in black: black tunic and trousers like the others, but also black socks and loafers, even a black-faced watch. He then spoke in a very calm voice, "I hope you are alone, Nick? I presume you do not have a wire, right?" Even before Nick could answer, he got frisked professionally. These men looked extremely intimidating.

"He is waiting for you," the man with the hair said. One of the shaven men knocked on the door three times, slowly. Marcus opened the door himself, still wearing his chinchilla fur coat and his Sponge Bob boxers on. He wore no trousers, Timberland boots and had sleepy red eyes with bulging bags underneath them. He smelled of alcohol and cigar smoke. He looked confused, lost – lonely. The unshaven money magnet stared at the skinny young man in front of him. Nick just stood in the hallway and strained his eyes looking back at him. His first up-close physical impression of the billionaire was that he had a fleshy face, pale blue eyes and bore an unsettling resemblance to the penguin in Batman.

"You wanted to see me?"

"Well, don't just stand there. Come in, you plonker." Marcus spoke with a funny English accent.

Both men entered the vast penthouse. Nick instantly felt as if he was in another world. The place was spotless, clean and vast, yet decorated with numerous unusual objects: over-the-top vases, statues, paintings he recognized from Paris, big windows, gargoyles, and an enviable view of New York.

"Cognac?" Marcus offered the young man. "Coffee would be better," Nick politely answered. "Are you scared?" Marcus asked. "Intrigued would be a better word to describe how I'm feeling," Nick retorted. "Well, you should be. I chop people's heads off. I kill beasts for fun. I grab the bull by the horns." Marcus handed Nick a glass of *Frapin Cuvée 1888*. "Here, drink! It's a seven-thousand bottle."

Nick took the drink as they headed into his personal office. There, he stumbled upon a vast library of books - hundreds upon hundreds of books. Nobody makes five billion dollars without knowing a thing or two about everything. He also noticed hideous animal trophy heads stuck on the wall: lion, bears, deer, brama bulls and leopards.

Every time Marcus looked at the orphan, he felt more and more insignificant and understood less and less how Dr Pierre-Clavert could recommend someone who seemed so unworldly. He mentioned that *"this kid has magical powers"*. How difficult it might have been to pretend that he felt perfectly at ease talking to someone who was his inferior. "You see this? That fucker right there almost got my arse, but I shot him right in the neck." Marcus touched his torso, which bore a scar, and pointed to the lion. "I wear one of his teeth around my neck now. I inherited his soul, his strength, his instincts, his pride, his roar. I defeated him. So now what was his is mine. Now sit." Nick, petrified, did as he was told. The man in front of him was more powerful than him. He was ruthless. "Drink! I don't trust a man who can't drink." Nick took a meager sip. His hand was shaking. "Good. Can I trust you?" Marcus asked. "Why am I here?" Nick asked. "I was told you have magical powers. Is that true?" Marcus probed some more. "I have listening powers," Nick replied. "I don't want you to listen; I want you to tell me something I don't already know. I want you to tell me the truth. All the whores I've slept with listened to me. My wife, my ex-wives, my employees, my driver, the mayor, the congressmen even the president of this bloody country listens to what I have to say and usually does I say. I'm surrounded by yes-men. I'm the most powerful and influential man on earth. But nobody dares tell me the truth. So I want you to tell me the truth. Can you do that?" Marcus added. "If you give me time, I could," Nick answered with a perplexed look. "Well, I've got some bad news for you, young man. This is only going to happen once. You don't have much time; you only have today. I only give myself one day in the year to play victim, to feel sorry for myself, to blame others. Tomorrow, I will be back chopping heads because that is what I do. So you better have your magical tricks on you today Harry-fucking-Potter." Marcus said aggressively. "Well, in that case you don't need me around. It looks like you've got everything figured out. Oh, and by the way using profanity in order to express yourself is a sign of weakness. It is crass and shows poor education, upbringing and probable emotional problems and difficulty relating to people," Nick answered.

He stood up, his face stern and serious, and started walking towards the front door.

"Hold on right there young man, I just wanted to see if you had some bollocks." Marcus exclaimed, smiling. "Some what? Bollocks?" Nick asked confused. "Yes, bollocks. Balls. Take a seat. Have another drink. I want to tell you a story." Nick returned to his seat silently with an air of relief on his face. He smiled and took another sip as Marcus started telling him the story of a traveler.

"Imagine yourself a traveler. What would you need to be happy? A comfortable seat? Sounds reasonable, right? How can you be a happy traveler, after all, if you're crowded for hours in a tight, severely cramped space? Actually, you can be a happy traveler in a tight cramped space. Better yet, you can be a happy traveler in a tight, cramped space even if you're soaked and shivering. You wouldn't mind one bit that damp and lack of space if you had been shipwrecked and just spent an hour treading water. You would be happy beyond belief to find any space at all no matter how tight in a lifeboat. You would shiver and smile. Now imagine yourself flying high above those ice cold waters, sitting comfortably in an airline aisle seat. You have plenty of room to stretch your legs and arms. No one is sitting next to you, or in front or behind. Sitting in your infinite comfort you strike up a conversation with the passenger across the aisle. He seems even happier than you are. You ask him why. You learn that he had found a fantastic deal for his ticket. He paid

one-third of what you paid. Suddenly, despite your comfort, you don't feel happy at all."

"That's a beautiful anecdote, Mr Hammond. So tell me, how I can help you?" Nick asked.

"What I want you to tell me is why we can't have everything in life. Why can't we have the best of both worlds? Why can't we have total freedom?" Marcus asked.

"Well, with the influence and power you tell me you possess, I would presume that you have the best of both worlds already. Whatever those worlds are. I would presume that you are free to do whatever you want, wish and please. Would I be audacious with my presumptions?" Nick answered.

"That's the problem young man. After all my living on this earth, having gotten what I thought I wanted – I have realized that total freedom does not exist. The only freedom that exists is the freedom to choose anything you like and then commit yourself to that decision." Marcus said.

"Are you saying that you chose poorly?" Nick asked again.

"I'm reconsidering my pursuit of wealth. Just for today," Marcus answered, lowering his eyes.

There was a long pause, which he followed with a question: "What's your take on money, young man?"

"I think that no one, at least no one who claims to be leading a rational life, pursues wealth simply to become wealthier. As individuals and as societies we treat wealth as a means to an end. We strive to become more productive, to create more wealth, only because we believe that wealth, at some level, can improve our lives, can make us in a word, happier." Nick answered in a stern voice.

The orphan continued by explaining how if those who fawned over fortunes were right, if letting wealth accumulate was indeed the prime prescription for a healthy vigorous society, we ought today to be enjoying a new golden age. Never before, after all, have grand fortunes accumulated as prodigiously as they have over recent decades, at least not in modern times. Our economy, given their awesome accumulation, ought to be vibrant and full of opportunities at every turn. Our enterprises should be generating wealth at extraordinary rates. We ourselves ought to be feeling stoked and energetic, confident that our hard work will be duly rewarded. Compassion ought to be flowing for the unfortunate; the arts ought to be blooming. We should be feeling absolutely terrific about ourselves and our country. But we aren't.

"So what went wrong? Where did I go wrong?" Marcus asked. "Greed, selfishness, avarice, love for excess, fear, craving, love for material things but mainly love of self," Nick answered without hesitation.

It's amazing how people can be so lonely. These days you can be living in a neighborhood without seeing the neighbors at all. Your closest friends or family could be several miles away. Everything is automated now: ATM bank machines, highway toll station without cashiers, gas stations without 'pumpists', or car wash without car washes. It is also amazing how most people are full of debt, taking loans to pay other past credits. They might have a nice fancy car (Mercedes or Jaguar) but live in a few-meter squared apartment.

*

When Marcus first arrived in NY he didn't have much. Maybe seven hundred dollars, but that was it: his life was summed up in seven hundred dollars. He had lost a good amount of money on gambling tables across the country and was wanted by two or three shylocks. So he had to make a move and decided to hide in the US. "Penniless, broke, fucking nothing," Marcus would say every time he narrated his success story. "I really worked my way up from the bottom - a true rags-to-riches story," he would sing, feeling all very proud.

Working as a credit analyst at Goldman Sachs in lower Manhattan, he quickly started making a name for himself, becoming the head trader on the high-yield desk at Goldman in just eighteen months. His primary focus was bankruptcies and special situations. He worked at Goldman for eight years, leaving in 1980, and started Hammond & Weisberg in early 1981 with his most trusted friend Carl.

Money started coming in. As he was serious about being wealthy, he started developing a sense of class far beyond that of the common man. He started enjoying things like polo, croquet and collecting ascots. He loved horses and all things equestrian. He owned a proper collection of riding boots, flared riding pants and a helmet reminiscent of Marvin the Martian. Horse-riding may at first appear a frivolous pastime, but one must move beyond the literal interpretation and realize that it is in fact a metaphor for success, as many wealthy patrons believe they have pulled themselves up by the bootstraps to overcome humble beginnings. Once he got into that mindset, he looked for other symbols: the cufflinks, the suspenders, the doormen, then sailing. He even tried producing a movie.

He always tried to play it very loose. He never carried a briefcase, tried not to schedule too many meetings and always let his door open at work as he firmly believed that no one could be imaginative or entrepreneurial if one had too much structure.

Nevertheless, it was Marcus's do-whatever-it-takes attitude that had made him one of the most powerful men in the world today. Convinced of the economic opportunities of the Big Apple, Marcus quickly applied his peerless understanding of numbers and art of negotiation. He watched and studied successful people and those who had failed. The one thing he saw more than any other trait in the successful people was that they never gave up.

CHAPTER SEVENTEEN

The two men were sitting silently in the rich man's office. Classical music was softly playing in the background as Marcus puffed on his cigar, blowing smoke rings into the warm air. Nick was playing with a prism that usually sat on the boss's desk as daylight was starting to peep through the gigantic windows. They were each in their own zone yet enjoying each other's company. Marcus then looked at the orphan and asked him, "Can wealth actually bring happiness? And if wealth can bring happiness, does that mean that still more wealth can bring yet more happiness?"

"Many very rich men are unhappy, Mr Hammond," Nick replied, still playing with the prism. "I told you to tell me things I did not already know." Marcus replied getting annoyed. Nick put the prism back on the desk, took another sip of the very expensive cognac, and answered "It's pretty hard to tell what does bring happiness. Poverty and wealth have both failed."

"Are you happy young man?" Marcus asked. "Compared to what? We define our happiness by our position, and we define our position by comparing ourselves to others or to ourselves at an earlier stage in our lives. Look at it this way: if you drive a Mercedes and I have to walk, that is a radical difference in lifestyle. But if you drive a Mercedes and I drive a Hyundai, it's a big deal. It's actually a monstrously big deal. Luxury affects everyone, even those who don't want to be affected. I wonder everyday why we put so much faith in the power of stuff to make us happy. People push ever harder for a satisfaction that always seems to elude them. They are trapped. So I have made my life's mantra not to get trapped in the cycle. Now, tell me why are you unhappy sir?"

"My wealth has come to burden me heavily on all aspects of my life – from the search for meaningful relationships to ambition to achieve. I am never sure of what I see. Money and fame rather than affection or love seem to attract people to me. So I have become wary of any intimate relationship, and find intimacy in my fortune. Money is my first and only love. It has, however, made me so lonely. That is why a couple of years ago, I gave my only daughter a big chunk of her inheritance. But she has not reciprocated in love or forgiveness." Marcus answered.

*

Marcus offered Nick some breakfast. During the meal, Nick told the maverick a fable he was once told when he was still a child back in his little town in Burundi about the dangers of excess. It went like this:

There are two ways of beating a drum…

Once upon a time there was a drummer living in a small country village.
    He heard there was going to be a fair in the city, so he decided to go there and earn some money by playing his drums. He took his son along to accompany him when playing music written for two set of drums.

The two drummers, father and son, went to the fair. They were very successful. Everyone liked their drum-playing and gave generously to them. When the fair was over, they began their trip back home to their little village.

On the way they had to go through a dark forest. It was dangerous because of muggers who robbed the travelers.

The drummer boy wanted to protect his father and himself from the muggers, so he beat his drums as loudly as he could, without stopping. The more noise the better, he thought. The drummer man took his son aside. He explained to him that when large groups passed by, especially royal processions, they were in the habit of beating drums. They did this at regular intervals, in a very dignified manner, as if they feared no one. They would beat a drum roll, remain silent, then beat another, then remain silent, then beat again with a flourish, and so on and so forth. He told his son to do likewise to fool the muggers into thinking there was a powerful lord passing by.

But the boy ignored his father's advice. He thought he knew best that more noise, the better.

Meanwhile, a gang of muggers heard the boy drumming. At first they thought it must be a powerful rich man approaching with heavy security. But then they heard the drumming continue in a wild fashion without stopping. They realized that it sounded frantic like a frightened little dog barking at a calm big dog. So they went to investigate and found only the father and son. They beat them up, took all their hard earned money, and escaped into the forest.

Marcus, intrigued by the young man's wisdom, asked him what the moral of the story was. Nick explained that overdoing always leads to a downfall.

*

It was about 9am. Nick needed to get to work. Marcus

thanked the orphan for his time and encouraged him to continue writing books that helped people's souls. He then removed Nick's novel from of his safe and asked him to personally sign it. Nick, feeling honored, did so with a big smile on his face. He then left the penthouse.

On his way to work he thought about selfishness and stubbornness. Greed or avarice is an excessive desire to acquire or possess more than one needs or deserves, especially with respect to material wealth. Greed, like lust and gluttony, is a sin of excess. Greed is inappropriate expectation. Greed is the tendency to selfish craving, grasping and hoarding. Craving is a delusional state of seeking happiness through acquiring material things. The person with greed is driven by a fundamental sense of deprivation, of something lacking within, and becomes fixated on seeking comfort by getting the one thing that will eliminate that feeling. That one thing could be money, power, sex, food, attention, knowledge - just about anything. But it will be the one thing on which their entire greed complex is fixated. The greedy person's basic strategy is to dedicate himself to acquiring as much as possible of that thing. The function of greed is to bind us to material things and so cloud our minds to all higher values. It ties us to the baser thing on earth. As lust binds us to the animal plane, so greed binds us to the mineral plane, on step lower. Hence, greed is even baser than lust. It makes for us a god of gold and silver and jewels. It identifies us with them by fixing our attention and affections upon them. The end result is slavery to them. Wealth then becomes master, instead of servant like all the other passions; it slowly forges its chains about us.

A greedy person is the result of a foolish and feeble mind; he or she is happy just thinking about his or her wealth, and will continuously be occupied in this desire to possess material items. Greed takes a person away from peace, from his or her religious, moral and social duties. The desire to own items purely because others own them, the desire to own material items that belong to others are all examples of greed.

LUCY HAMMOND

-THE HEIRESS-

CHAPTER EIGHTEEN

The restaurant was full and vibrating with a warm festive mood. It was summer, and spirits where high and moods were in sync with the season. Lucy and her date, were dining at a restaurant called Jean-Georges in Central Park - West. It was listed as one of the best restaurants in the world. A meal there could cost almost $200 per person without the wine of course. Individuals like Donald Trump, Michael Bloomberg and Rudy Giuliani dined there occasionally. New York City was feeling slightly better and Lucy Hammond was on a romantic date.

She'd been asked out by Axel Manning, a young entrepreneur who owned a boutique hotel in the village. They were having a rather good time, talking about various issues and drinking sweet red wine as they engaged fervently in their desserts: tiramisu for the lady and an authentic Austrian strudel for the gentleman. As they chatted, Lucy kept looking and smiling at something or someone behind him, which made him look back to see what she was looking at. There was nobody behind him. He never thought too much about it as he kept talking, trying not to lose his train of thought. He kept asking her questions. "So tell me something that most people don't know about you."

"Hmmm, let me see, I cry when I watch movies." Lucy answered, embarrassed.

"Really? I wouldn't have thought that about you. You had such a tough demeanor when I saw you at the firm," Axel retorted, surprised.

Lucy's venture capitalist firm had worked with Axel

on his boutique hotel project two years prior to their romantic date. He wasn't their client anymore, but still had good relations with the firm, as the whole concept of boutique hotels was gaining a lot of attention in the market. He was a bachelor - single, handsome, and desired by women. He was regarded as a "*keeper*" and was headed for great success at a fast pace. Lucy was inevitably attracted to the idea of him because she was passionately chasing power. Celebrity is an aphrodisiac. It is good for a woman's ego to be with a man who has chosen her even though he had the pick of many others. She understood that as a woman, she would acquire the status (even some of the power) of the man she would choose to be with. She had noticed how girls could be treated as two entirely different people just because they had changed escorts. Thus she had to choose right.

Little did she know, he was quite naïvely oblivious to all this attention on him and did not get involved in devious ego-tripping power games. He was dyslexic and had attended special schools in his childhood. He was very small compared to his age mates growing up, so he spent a lot of time on his own while the others played sports and spent his childhood working hard overcoming these so-called disabilities, ultimately forging a character of strength, patience and unmatched focus. His ultimate essence was of progress.

"Tell me what you hate most about people?" Axel kept asking.

"Well, I don't hate, period. Hate is such a strong word," Lucy answered with attitude, proud of herself. "I mean, what character trait do you despise the most in a person?" Axel readjusted his question. "I would have to say arrogance - when someone feels, thinks or acts as if he was better or more intelligent than everybody else.

It's such a turn-off. What about you? What character trait do you despise the most?" Lucy asked. "Well, for me dishonesty would be the one I despise the most. Nothing good - I mean absolutely nothing good - can come out of lies."

They chatted for about an hour, talking about their childhoods or crazy times in college – the usual stuff people talk about when they are getting to know each other. She idealized celebrity magazines, especially the people in them. They looked smiling and content, what she failed to realize was that the people having fun at that moment when the picture was taken would have a different story later the same night or morning. Most probably, those celebrities asked themselves what they had to do in order to continue appearing in those same magazines. How could they disguise the fact they no longer had enough money to support their luxurious lifestyle? How best could they manipulate their luxurious lifestyle to make it seem even more luxurious than everyone else? Lucy was a slave of fame.

Finishing their dinner, they decided to go for a late movie together to cap off the night. As they stood up after paying the bill, Axel caught a glimpse of what Lucy kept staring at the whole evening. Apparently it was a mirror. It didn't click in his mind at first, but she was actually looking at and admiring herself the whole time he was talking to her. He never could have understood how such things could tell so much about a person. He remained silent.

Lucy had just ended a three-year romantic relationship with a man due to issues of power and control. She wanted to wear the pants and treated him almost as a servant. She was always calculating who did what for whom, and what was fair and equitable. The more successful he became, the more threatened she felt. She was losing control and was not scared to use sex in order to keep it.

As Jacqueline Kennedy once said: *"There are two kinds of women: those who want power in the world and those who want power in bed."*

Lucy wanted both…

Vanity got the best of her. She was pretty and hard-working, and said all the right things at the right time and the right way. She basically told you what you wanted to hear. She was in love with herself. She spent her days trying to hold back time, always checking the scales, because she thought love depended on it. Shallow waters.

She was in a delusion about her importance, with no intrinsic respect for others. She was out to get hers. Whatever the circumstance, she had to know what was in it for her. She wanted to be the best, but she got ahead of herself and actually started believing that she was the best - better than the rest (whoever 'the rest' is). She wanted to be visible, present, and impossible to ignore. She really wanted to be a *'Zahir'*. She wanted to be someone or something that, once others came into contact with her, would gradually occupy their every thought, until they could not think of nothing else – frightening.

She had good grades at school growing up. She was smart and knew it. She had many so-called friends and knew how to manipulate them. It really fed her ego. What made things worse was that she found joy in flaunting all her perceived positive and enviable attributes and made sure that everybody was aware of them. Oddly enough, everybody manages to find themselves good-looking or handsome, but she really believed that she was the prettiest.

Her prideful soul suggested that she could not admit her vanity or her faults. She had an excess of pride and tried to conceal her faults. With her poor understanding, she asserted herself with pride, ego and low habits, desiring to be recognized. She was in search of power. She needed to be significant.

In her work environment, she almost inevitably thought first and foremost of herself. She understood that the world was a harsh and competitive place, and she had to look after her own interests. Even when she acted for the greater good, she was often unconsciously motivated by the desire to be liked by others and to have her image enhanced in the process. She had no shame in it, but because being self-interested did not make her feel or appear noble, she went out of her way to disguise her self-interest. She was a slave to luxury, to the appearance of luxury, to the appearance of the appearance of luxury. Nevertheless, those who are the most self-absorbed will often surround their actions with a moral or saintly aura, or will make a show of supporting all of the right causes.

She made it her motto to play with appearances and master the art of deception. She was many different people by wearing the mask that the day and the moment required. She always concealed her intentions. She knew very well that if the people she was deceiving had the slightest suspicion as to her intentions, all would be lost. So she used false sincerity, sent ambiguous signals and set up misleading objects of desire. She was coquette.

In reality she had an unconscious inferiority complex because pride is always a compensation for feelings of inferiority and inadequacy. This inferiority complex is a basic emotion present in all humans, and it heavily influences their actions. She was also passive aggressive, and the root cause of this was her fear of direct confrontations – the emotions that a conflict could churn up and the loss of control that ensued. So because of this fear she looked for indirect means of getting her way, making her attacks subtle enough so that it was hard to figure out what was going on, while giving herself control of the dynamic. Procrastination on projects, showing up late, or making offhand comments designed to upset people are all common forms of low-level passive aggression.

Nevertheless, Lucy had major "daddy issues". Her father Marcus Hammond was one of America's richest people. Most pundits would have believed that she grew up in wealth and all kinds of unimaginable luxuries, but that was not really the case. Actually, it was rather the opposite. She was about four years old when her parents divorced, after which her mother refused any alimony money or any kind of funds from her ex-husband. Marcus wasn't exactly fighting to pay hefty sums of money for he loved his money too much. Lucy therefore grew up like most children in the western world: with a single mom and on-off stepdads. Marcus was absent in Lucy's childhood. She went to public schools and carpooled with the neighbors' kids. Her mother managed to find a job as a secretary at an advertisement company on Madison Avenue, as she did not want to go back to her parents in Philadelphia with her tail between her legs. They'd been against her marriage to Marcus from the get-go. She did not have a college degree, so things were tough, and she did not make it easier by getting involved with worthless men. Lucy witnessed all of this and vowed to be someone of importance, to not fit the role of traditional women, to be an independent woman. She needed to be significant.

"Femininity is socially constructed," she would say. She believed that there was no way in hell she could ever be appreciated by her friends, peers and parents as a mere homemaker. She dreamed of the lunch in the executive dining rooms, police escorts on the way to the theatre, celebrities present for all occasions, a personal wine cellar at one or several restaurants. She would fantasize about and take pleasure in conquering powerful men, thereby making them pathetic and human. Seeing a once-feared executive pad around in shorts to bring her breakfast in bed gave her a feeling of accomplishment.

Living in New York City with a struggling single mom who got abused and manipulated by insignificant men, while knowing that she had a mythical millionaire father somewhere in the city, really tinkered with her understanding of life. It was NYC, for crying out loud. Society constantly induced in her a tendency to compare, and an inferiority was born – born out of endless comparison. This kind of inferiority complex that is deeply imbedded with a person does not easily show itself externally. A person with this kind of complex tries to hide their complex by putting on a bluff or façade over that which they lack. Usually people who act as though they are superior to others exhibit a complex that needs to be specially hidden.

CHAPTER NINETEEN

The gathering marked the debut of first time author Nicholas Jordan for the signing of his best-seller *Cleaning Up the Ghetto – Tales of the Minority*. The venue was the legendary 'The Stand' bookstore on Broadway. There were a few handshakes, a few letters, gifts, comments and eye contact, but mainly a feeling of solidarity. Champagne and canapés were served. Among the fifty-plus guests were Michel and Sigourney, of course, Mr Parker (Levy and Stan's father), his manager and a few of his buddies and work colleagues. Oddly enough, Lucy was also present, acting all giddy. She had reached out to him soon after he published the book, acting all friendly and extra nice out of the blue. Celebrity is an aphrodisiac.

Nick returned to the table after a thirty-minute break, full of energy and still signing books even though the shop had closed its doors and the queue was dwindling. There were about forty people left inside, who soon became thirty, eleven, eight, then just five. It was time to go out to eat, drink and share the excitement of the day and describe some of the strange things that had happened during the signing. However, it was also going to be a farewell party for Nick as he was leaving the firm and New York for Massachusetts. He was going to attend Harvard University to earn his masters degree in theology. This promised to be a memorable night.

After all the guests had left, Michel and Sigourney, Mr. Parker, the publisher and bookstore manager all cheered and congratulated Nick for his great work.

They drank more champagne and let Nick go celebrate his farewell party with his peers. The party was organized by Lucy. They decided to walk to their designated place of celebration at a bar called 'Broadway Dive Bar'. As they walked on New York's streets during the summer with its stinky clouds of hot meat air wafting off the street carts, the many tourists, the walking tours, the many concerts or outdoor film festivals. The city looked extremely alive and jovial. Nick and Lucy's arms were intertwined, and they trotted along as if they had no worries. Nick was feeling slightly more excited than usual, and started talking emotionally:

"I shall never forget you, Broadway
Your golden and calling lights.

I'll remember you long.
Tall-walled river of rush and play.

Hearts that know you hate you,
And lips that have given you laughter
Have gone to their ashes of life and its roses,
Cursing the dreams that were lost
In the dust of your harsh and trampled stones."

"That is beautiful, Nick. Did you compose this poem?" Lucy asked, wooed by his words. "It's a poem written by Carl Sandburg. He is talking of New York. It's called "Broadway"," Nick answered with a sad tone.

"Well, you delivered it very beautifully nonetheless." Lucy said. "I love this poem because it makes me think so much of my home country and my family, especially on a day like this one. I wish my dad was still around to see all this success I am achieving and the man I am becoming." Nick added. "Perhaps being fatherless has provided us immense obstacles in our paths, but we will continue to be independent and strong people. I for one am reaching for the sky and I will accomplish my goals. But I also understand that I need to surround myself with positive male figures like you did with Michel and Mr Parker, but especially with my significant other," Lucy replied. "Yes, but you are lucky to still have your father around," Nick retorted. "Lucky? Lucky was never a word I identified with as a child. I never considered myself lucky. In my adolescence and even into my adulthood, I suffered many struggles as a result of not having a father. I love my mother very much, and I am extremely grateful to her for dedication in raising me by herself, but her unconditional love could not fill the void left by not having a father in my life. I will never forget me asking my mother where Daddy was when I was about four or five. My mother responded politely and did not bad mouth my father or what I later perceived to be his devastating and decimating abandonment. She told me that I had Grandpa, Uncle Ben and my cousins, who all loved me and who I could look at as my daddies. So I had several fathers, men that I adopted as my daddies and who in turn gave me unconditional love and protection. However, this love did not fill the emptiness of not having a relationship with my biological father."

Lucy picked up her phone, changed her tone of voice and started talking. All the while Nick was pondering what Lucy had just told her. He thought about girls and their daddy issues. A father instills not only his beliefs in his children, but specifically shapes his daughter's Feminity - a huge part of her identity. More notably, this influence is reflected in the daughter's own romantic relationships. Perhaps the abandoned daughter searches for a man who will protect her.

*

As soon as they reached the bar, Lucy changed her demeanor and the show began. Her act was set in gear; she was unrecognizable. She saw her friend Dahlia and screamed irrationally out of joy, hugging her for about five minutes. One would have thought that long-lost friends had just reunited after years apart, but they had seen each other just the day before.

Dahlia had invited a few of her friends from the UN, where they held high positions working in the human rights and justice section. Lucy's cousin Melina from her mother's side was also invited. The majority of Marcus & Weisberg (Nick's colleagues) were also present - notably Terrance and Steven who represented the traders - and Jackson who was responsible for I.T. Lucy did what she did best: she worked the room like she owned the place. She started to interact enthusiastically with the invited guests, taking cues from their reactions and adapting her words and body language to elicit her audience's attention and enthusiasm. She knew how to spot the people who were most likely to respond positively.

One should understand that most people are like open books. They say what they feel, blurt out their opinions at every opportunity and constantly reveal their plans and intentions. Lucy believed that honesty was actually a blunt instrument that bloodied more than it cut. She understood that it is much more prudent to tailor your words, telling people what they want to hear rather than the coarse and ugly truth of what you feel or think. Deception was always in her mind, her best strategy. Everyone wears a mask in society; we pretend to be more sure of ourselves than we are. We do not want other people to glimpse that doubting self within us. In truth, our egos and personalities are much more fragile than they appear to be; they cover up feelings of confusion and emptiness.

After engaging all the invited guests in conversation, she settled with her group of so-called friends. It was funny to see how competition walks hand in hand with pride and envy, because most women seek the admiration and attention of other women. As little girls, and later teenagers, most if not all of them wanted to be popular or part of a popular group of girls. Gaining acceptance and approval was crucial to their self-worth, and as women they still had that desire. Nick stood in between them, trying to make conversation. He felt a bit of discomfort at these women's pettiness, and somewhat got disappointed by their lack of support, because today was his day. He recognized in their behavior the all-too–familiar pattern of women comparing and measuring themselves against other women. When we compare, we find difference, and difference often feels threatening. Women do not readily confide to each other their frustrations. They often fall into the trap of inauthentic niceness. I presume that the popular saying, '*the hardest thing about being a woman is having women friends*' is true. It is quite sad to see how certain women allow other women to define who they are.

Nick heart sickened, and he moved on and went to chat with the fellows – maybe there he would find more camaraderie. There with his fellow men, he talked about broad issues like the book signing, the message of the book, the reasons why he was leaving the firm and why he had decided to study theology. However, he noticed that they were hearing, not listening.

Whenever they expressed themselves, they had a *"me first"* agenda, justifying their every story, looking for reinforcement, attacking everything that could bolster and strengthen their *"me-centered"* mind-set. They continually compared themselves to others, craving respect and recognition from others. Basically, they were making a point to showcase their brilliance.

Feeling out of place, Nick went to the bathroom, got to a sink and splashed his face with cold water. The tap still running, he looked at himself in the mirror and thought, *Admiration is usually at odds with love. If we seek to be admired, we seek an audience. An audience lacks the close involvement that generates love. In wanting admiration, we want to be perfect. Love, however, tolerates and even welcomes imperfections. People and situations actually control how we feel, what we think and how we act, all through the ego. If one is honest and looks deep inside oneself, one will see that this is completely true. Watch carefully how we go through life reacting versus acting. It is the great irony that the ego actually creates the problem it attempts to solve. Only when we see this can we begin our escape from its grip.*

But how will I feel good? Isn't having a good self-esteem healthy? How can I live without some reassurance that I am good and worthwhile? Who will I be?" he pondered. Magically, his reflection in the mirror answered him: *I beg of you to see that your current ideas of good are false. For every false good there is always a false bad in equal proportions and equal intensity. True good has none of that. It is always good, all of the time. This is what you have in place of that which you left behind. Don't look for anything in what the world calls self-esteem. Self-esteem is a misnomer. It suggests that I, who lacks esteem, shall be in charge of gaining it. If I do not have it, I must get it elsewhere. If I get it elsewhere, it is no longer mine. If other people's approval of my identity and personality are where I get my esteem, isn't it true that they can take it away with disapproval? What self is there in that?* Nick, in a trance, asked his reflection: *What about gaining self-esteem in doing good things and being a good person?* His reflection replied: *Please see that doing good and being good are still reflections in your mind of how the world sees you. Furthermore, what you may think is good may be considered bad by another. What will you do then, when they show their disapproval?*"

Praise generally does harm. Ever so slowly, the emphasis shifts from the joy of the creative process to the love of attention and to our ever-inflating ego. Without realizing it, we alter and shape our work to attract the praise that we crave. We fail to understand the element of luck that always goes into success. We often depend on being in the right place at the right time. Instead, we come to think that our brilliance has naturally drawn our success and attention, as if it were indeed fated. Once the ego inflates, it will only come back to earth through some jarring failure, which will equally scar us. To avoid this fate, one must have some perspective. There are always greater geniuses out there than ourselves.

*

Standing there in the bathroom, Nick understood that pride and vanity are the excessive love of self. It is the desire to be more important or attractive than others. It is failing to acknowledge the good work of others. Pride and ego do not let us progress. When we make mistakes we will not admit them. In our hearts we have the thought *"there is none greater than me."* Lucy got swayed by the intoxication of power. She took pride in her beauty and thought that she could do anything.

PRIDE! This is the emotion that arises when an individual judges themselves abnormally. It ultimately means that one's self-esteem is low. No one wants less power; everyone wants more. The feeling of having no power over people and events was generally unbearable to Lucy. When she felt helpless, she felt miserable. But it was dangerous for her to seem too power-hungry, to be overt with her power moves. She understood that she had to seem fair and decent. So she was subtle – congenial yet cunning, democratic yet devious. She required the ability to play with appearances, so she learned to wear many masks and keep a bag full of deceptive tricks. Consequently, she succeeded only in heaping more misery upon her own head.

In all fairness, we all have a self-image that is more flattering than the truth: we think of ourselves as more generous, selfless, honest, kindly, intelligent, or good-looking than in fact we are. It is extremely difficult for us to be honest with ourselves about our own limitations; we have a desperate need to idealize ourselves. Pride is always a compensation for feelings of inferiority and inadequacy. All problems including insecurity, financial trouble, bad habits and the like are not really problems at all until the ego gets a hold of them. If it were not for the ego, these issues and situations would pass right by you with no attention paid to them whatsoever. But the ego catches everything – everything! From every situation, the ego draws whatever it needs to give itself life. Every problem you have right now is no problem at all for your true self. But they are all big problems for the ego, just as it likes them to be. Problems, as they are, exist only because of resistance. The same is true with our emotions. The ego creates the problem with its resistance to letting the situation go and simply pass by. It feels its importance would be diminished by the lack of acknowledgment. It sees an opportunity to inflate itself.

The ego's chief aim is self-preservation. It will devour everything it can for nourishment. It calls to attract accolades, compliments and physical satisfaction at every turn. When devoid of those satisfactions, comparisons become the natural substitute. Am I better than he or she? Am I smarter, stronger and more successful than other people in the world? Do I consider some other person to be lacking in humility? These comparisons lead to a search for an identity. The question *"who am I?"* is misinterpreted by the ego as "what am I known for?" and more dangerously as *"what shall I be known for?"* At the command of the ego, you personally proceed to take on all kinds of absurd identities by what you do, what you say, and how you present yourself. Uniqueness is highly desirable to the ego because it has less competition and stands out in a crowd.

When you lose control or err because of it, the ego then blames the world for your trouble, furiously seeking someone or something to blame in order to ease the burden of fault, and even worse: the burden of guilt. In general the ego convinces you that the world puts unfair demands of you. It tells you that your spouse or employer or people unreasonably expect too much, but you had better not disappoint. It plays movies in your head of the consequences should you fail to comply. When you cannot take it any more, you lash out at those entities and create a mess out of what was only an image in your mind to begin with.

Feeling good about oneself and having high self-esteem are important to most people. Self-esteem, as the world views it, could really be called ego esteem. The widely accepted concept is just another way for the ego to stake its claim on you. Nick understood that the best thing anyone could do to help themselves was to seek, from this point forward, true esteem. One will need to be willing to let go of the identities the ego has created. One would have to cease trying to be somebody. As a matter of fact, do your true esteem a favor and work hard to be nothing at all. Don't perpetuate your current condition by being that condition. Say to yourself *"that is the ego feeling those emotions, not my true self."*

Nick returned to his party, keeping all his thoughts to himself and just listened to everyone else talk about themselves. He could not stand being there, but managed to stomach the evening regardless. As more drinks were shared, egos got bigger; the truth became more glaring to some as the alcohol took its toll. The group decided to end the night in a nightclub. Nick, however, went home and starting packing, as the next day he would travel to Massachusetts. Maybe the grass was greener there.

THE LETTER

"Becoming Father Nickolas"

CHAPTER TWENTY ONE

The Degree of Master in Theology was written in bold and golden letters. Nick stared at his degree for a good ten minutes trying to fathom what all this could mean. The idea of him actually going through with his secret goal frightened him to the point of smoking three cigarettes in a row. *Maybe I should write another book*, he quietly thought. *I should write a story about a boy who loses his family in an awful genocide. This boy is filled with hate and blames everyone for all the bad and hurt in his life. This boy should become a priest. That would be a good twist.* Nick snickered.

He had just spent two years in Massachusetts at Harvard University. He had just come back to New York. Feeling restless in his little apartment, disturbed by his thoughts and his indecisions, he decided to write a poem about forgiveness. His mind was not still, though, and threw away all the pages he wrote. He decided to read a book to change his thoughts, but threw it on his bed after reading the first three pages. He received a dozen phone calls, but ignored all of them. He got about ten messages, but did not bother either to read them. His phone kept blowing up. Something must have happened, but he was in the process of letting go. He decided to go to the movies – all he wanted was to think about something mundane.

He put his Nike Air Jordans on, over worn jeans, a white t-shirt and a black turtle neck pull-over, with his reading glasses and his faithful NY baseball cap. He nonchalantly walked down the stairs. He stumbled upon some teenagers kissing in the staircase. They did not stop as he passed them by. As he walked down the building, he encountered an altercation between two women. He did not bother taking up the role of peacemaker as he usually did. He walked past them. "Ah, New York!" he exclaimed."

On his way to the movies, he passed by Corpus Christi Catholic Church on 121st. He could not help but stop and look at it. No matter what he did, he was constantly reminded of what he was most afraid of. He felt powerful emotions that enticed him to enter the church. He removed his cap and immediately felt at peace. He lit a candle and made a promise, a sacred ritual promise: to forgive - to forgive God, to forgive himself, to forgive the world. He would have to let go.

He suddenly felt guilty. Maybe it was just some emotions related to being inside the house of God. Nevertheless, he was under the impression that his sins would never be forgiven if not confessed. He did not hesitate and went toward the confessional box. He pulled aside the curtain and entered and sat down. He heard a priest come in and begin the confession with the prayer of the sign of the cross. "Father, forgive me, for it has been a very long time since I've been to confession. Actually, I have never been to confession. OK, let me start over: Father, forgive me for I have never been to confession in my life."

A moment of silence… Nick could hear some heavy breathing. It was awkward, as he had chosen an anonymous confession.

"Go on," The priest added in a low voice added. "What do I do now?" Nick asked. "First, you have to examine your conscience honestly and thoroughly. It is of great importance for you to be able to receive the sacrament of confession." The priest said. "I have,

Father. I have been examining my conscience for the past ten years father. I even went to the extent of studying theology and the Bible." Nick spoke. "Please do tell the mortal sins you have committed," The priest followed. "I have committed the sin of envy, Father. I envy my friends, my neighbors, and my work colleagues. I am sure if my brothers were alive, I would envy their traits too. I have committed the sin of anger and fury. I have secretly been bitter for the past ten years. Things have not gone my way, and I blame everyone else including God. I have committed the sin of gluttony, for I fell in love with French red wine and foie gras – the finer things in life. I indulge myself. I smoke marijuana and cigarettes. I cannot stop. I have committed the sin of lust, for I am obsessed with my dreams and goals. Obsessed with the pursuit of success and perfection. This is probably the reason why I cannot find a woman whom I deem worthy of my time and love. I have committed the sin of sloth, for I have been secretly depressed, and find no joy in things that I once found enjoyable, making me cynical and pessimistic. I have committed the sin of greed, for I have made quite a sum of money with the sales of my book. I have made enough money for me not to have to work for the next ten years, yet I want more and I haven't used it in a positive way. I smoke my money, drink my money and just bought a Porsche. I don't even know how to drive. Lastly, I have committed the sin of pride, for I earnestly think highly of myself. I believe I am special, that I deserve better, that I am probably smarter than most people, that people should be aware of my greatness. I wrote a book, so now people should look at me differently, I should not wait in line no more, and people should recognize me in the streets. I am a show off." Nick started weeping.

"Son, let me tell you something about forgiveness

and of faith. The wounds from hurt incurred from loved ones or hurt or harm on your loved ones may leave you with lasting feelings of anger, bitterness or even vengeance. If you don't practise forgiveness, you might be the one who pays the most dearly. By embracing forgiveness, you can also embrace peace, hope, gratitude and joy. Consider how forgiveness can lead you down the path of physical, emotional and spiritual well-being. Forgiveness is a decision to let go. The act of forgiving does not come easy to most of us. Our natural instinct is to recoil in self-protection when we've been injured. We don't naturally overflow with mercy, grace and understanding when we've been wronged. Forgiveness is a choice we make through a decision of our will motivated by obedience to God and his command to forgive. This is where faith comes in to play. The beauty of faith is that you go out not knowing. But just believing, trusting without seeing or understanding. You can only manage to do that when you purify your heart and mind from the filth your flesh desires to consume. Once you have managed that, you leave out enough space for him to work."

"By him you mean God?" Nick asked.

"Yes. He is in all of us but we find ways to corner him in a hidden space in our souls where he has no room to work. He needs your permission for him to work in your life. But there are some days when you feel him or when we free him. Those moments only happen when you let go," The priest said.

"So you are saying that when I forgive, I free God in me?" Nick asked.

"Yes." The priest answered.

*

After the very enlightening talk with the priest, Nick

was dumbstruck and started walking aimlessly just outside the church. The words of the priest had shaken him. He slowly walked very thoughtfully to Central Park. He sat alone with a trance-like gaze. He started feeding squirrels, which usually relaxed him. He looked at the people around him: busy people, working overtime, worrying about their children, their husbands and wives, their careers, their degrees. They constantly thought of what they were going to do tomorrow. They lived in the future; their happiness was always in the future. They constantly thought of what they needed to buy, what they need to have in order not to feel less inferior. Nevertheless, nobody would admit to another person that they were unhappy. Most would say *"I'm fine"*, or *"I've got everything I ever wanted"*.

*

He took a yellow cab and went to Starbucks. There was a long line. *People in New York are crazy about coffee*, he thought to himself. After taking a sip, he slowly walked along 5TH Avenue. He went window-shopping at Saks and Century 21. He then ate a pizza, took the subway and walked to Brooklyn bridge to catch the sunset. He had tears in his eyes. Nevertheless, he looked inspired - better yet: emancipated. He had made a decision, one of letting go, because when you let go, when you have nothing more to lose, that is when you're given everything. When you cease to be who you are, you find yourself. When you experience humiliation and yet keep on walking, you are free to choose your destiny. He concluded that the energy of hatred won't get anybody anywhere, but the energy of forgiveness, which reveals itself through love, will transform everyone's life in a positive way.

He didn't want to go back to his tiny apartment quite yet. He decided to meet some friends at a bar, as a way to be sure, a way of not feeling too lonely. He chatted for about an hour. Though he was mostly silent, he just sat next to his friends listening to their various discussions and observing their body language, trying to see if it matched what they said. By talking about their lives, he came to realize that most people have experienced the same thing. And if we are not alone, then we have more strength to find out where we went wrong and have all the told to change direction. As he reached into his pocket to get some money to pay his tab, he found tickets to the Lion King on Broadway given to him by an acquaintance of his. He decided to have a go and see it, travelling to Broadway all alone. He went straight home after the show. He could not find any sleep, and started writing a letter, but he could not find the right words. He left the pen on the pad and lay on his bed. He received a text. He took a lot of his time to read it. It stated, "You are number 1 on NY's bestseller list. Congrats, son. Michel."

The news did not evoke any emotion. He remained extremely calm. He closed his eyes and thought about the confession: *I have made the choice because there is no other way to live. Nothing else makes sense, nothing else ever fits, nothing else ever works. So we pretend that everything is OK. So I have let go and just now believe. My work now is to live purely. I will not go and force-feed his mightiness and his truth to others because I am a practical man who seeks to manifest a being, a force, an energy, a GOD who is practical beyond my understanding. I will manifest him through my way of life, my conduct, the happiness in my face, voice, in my body language, and in my work. People will want to know what is my secret and I will let them know I let go and let him in.* He smiled and fell asleep immediately.

*

He woke up early, and went for a run around the lake in Central park. He followed the jog with a hearty all-American breakfast: pancakes and oatmeal. He loved pancakes. He went to the Metropolitan Museum and followed that with a visit to the opera. He took a late dinner at a Chinese restaurant. He returned to his apartment, and sat on his desk looking at the pen and pad, then wrote a letter to the Bishop. This was the letter that proved to the Bishop that Nickolas was ready to be ordained:

The world around us is far more complex than we can imagine. Human beings are complex creatures, and our circumstances are complex. From the moment a baby is born, as he catches sight of the light of the world at that particular moment he seeks to find himself and get hold of himself out of its confusion. With our limited senses and consciousness, we only glimpse a small portion of reality. Our problems need to be understood in context and in perspective.

We are by nature fearful and insecure creatures. We do not like what is unfamiliar or unknown. In childhood, liberation takes the direction of trying to get to the bottom of things, spying out the weak points of everybody and everything. It is well known that children have a sure instinct: they like to smash things, like to rummage through hidden corners, pry after what is covered up and try what we can do with everything. As we grow up, to compensate for the lack of curiosity we were born with, we assert ourselves with opinions and ideas that make us seem strong and certain making our society almost entirely dedicated to the celebration of the EGO. This is when morality comes into play. Almost all of us experience a split in our consciousness.

Societies use ideas about what is and is not moral to create values that serve them well. In almost all cultures morality is the definition of good and evil; vices and virtues. I purposely focus on the vices as they are the keys to any redemption.

In common usage a "vice" is a personal habit or social practice, or an aspect of human character of which we disapprove. On one hand, we understand the need to follow certain basic codes of behavior that have been in place for centuries. We try our best to live by them. However, as human beings, we are all prone to making mistakes. These mistakes stem from poor choices and bad decisions. Some things are done in ignorance, many as a function of bad behavior. Each time one makes a choice, one must be prepared to experience the consequences of that choice. However, we all have the opportunity to make new choices in our lives that will affect future generations. No matter how terrible we think we are, how bad we believe we have been, how low we think we have fallen, we can clean out our minds and begin again.

On the other hand, we also sense that the world has become infinitely more competitive than anything our parents or grandparents have known. Life involves constant battle and confrontation. This comes on two levels. On one level, we have desires and needs, our own interests that we wish to advance. In a highly competitive world, this means we must assert ourselves and even occasionally push people out of position to get our way. On the other level, there are always people who are more aggressive than we are. At some point they cross our path and try to block or to harm us. On both levels, playing offense and defense, we have to manage people's resistance and hostility. This has been the human drama since the beginning of history and no amount of progress will alter this dynamic. The only thing that has changed is how we handle these inevitable moments of friction in our lives.

The result of all this is that in order to get ahead in this world, we find ourselves being obliged to occasionally bend that moral code, to play with appearances, to hedge the truth and make ourselves look better, to manipulate a person or two to secure our position. The culture at large reflects this division. It emphasizes values of cooperation and decency, while titillating us constantly in the media with endless stories of those who have risen to the top by being bad and ruthless. We are both drawn to and repulsed by these stories. This split creates an ambivalence and awkwardness in our actions. We are not very good at being either good or bad.

Throughout recorded history we can detect patterns of human behavior that transcend culture and time, indicating certain universal features that belong to us as a species. Some of these traits are quite positive – for instance, our ability to cooperate with one another in a group – while some of them are negative and can prove destructive. Most of us have these negative qualities in mild doses. But in a group setting, there will inevitably be people who have one or more of these qualities to a high enough degree that they can become very destructive. We shall call these negative qualities the seven deadly sins.

You see, the cause of any sin or wrong action in this world is DESIRE. The common denominator of any sin is immaturity of the soul, which makes it incapable of relating, communicating and loving. In the broadest terms, sin is lack of LOVE. An immature person is never able to love. Anyone in that condition is selfish, egocentric, blind, and cannot understand others.

Immaturity means separateness. In separateness, one does not love and is therefore in 'sin'. This concept of sin, in psychological terms is neurosis. The only difference between the spiritual and psychological approach is that spiritual approach puts emphasis on the result, while the psychological approach shows the underlying causes and the different currents and components leading to separateness neurosis or sin.

Every individual we come across in life is unique, with his or her own energy, desires, and history. But wanting more control over people, our first impulse is generally to try to push them into conforming to our moods and ideas, into acting in ways that are familiar and comfortable to us. We cannot physically make events more predictable, but we can internally create a feeling of greater control by holding on to certain ideas and beliefs that give us a sense of consistency and order. This hunger for control, common to all of us, is the root of so many problems in life. Staying true to the same ideas and ways of doing things makes it that much harder for us to adapt to the inevitable changes in life. If we try to dominate a situation with some kind of aggressive action, this becomes our only option. We cannot give in, or adapt, or bide our time – that would mean letting go of our grip, and we fear that. Having such narrow options makes it hard to solve problems. Forcing people to do what we want makes them resentful – inevitably they sabotage us or assert themselves against our will. What we find is that our desire to micromanage the world around us comes with a paradoxical effect: the harder we try to control things in our immediate environment, the more likely we are to lose control in the long run.

Here is the truth: we are all in search of feeling more connected to reality – to other people, the times we live in, the natural world, our character, and our own uniqueness. Our culture increasingly tends to separate us from these realities in various ways. We indulge in drugs or alcohol, or engage in dangerous sports or risky behavior, just to wake ourselves up from the sleep of our daily existence and feel a heightened sense of connection to reality. In the end, however, the most satisfying and powerful way to feel this connection is by trying our sincere best to achieve union with GOD. In doing this work we are, in fact, knowing our true selves.

I am in awe of the gift and task entrusted to human beings through the priesthood. No human being can ever feel worth of such a gift or such a responsibility because we are human. There will be times when we fail, but our response to our weakness must be to cling ever more closely to God.

I am religiously serious, prayerful, socially adept, intellectually perceptive, I possess interior integrity, sound common sense, and habits hard work. However, I am also weak enough to be a priest. I am deficient enough so that I cannot ward off significant suffering from my life, so that I live with a certain amount of failure, so that I can feel what it is to be an average man. I have a history of confusion, of self-doubt, of interior anguish. I had to deal with fear, come to terms with frustrations and accept deflated expectations. Weakness more profoundly relates us to God, because it provides the arena in which his grace can be seen.

So here is how I am going to manage my concerns: the cause of God, the cause of Goodness, the cause of Mankind, of Truth, of Freedom, of Humanity, of Justice; further, the cause of my people, my motherland and finally even the cause of Mind. Only my cause is never to be a concern. I'm letting go. I forgive, for I want to be forgiven.

Shame on the egoist who thinks only of himself!

THE END

Author's Note

I wrote *Greener on the other side* between October 2012 and September 2013, while my family and I were building a beach resort. It has been the most grueling, yet exciting and most eye-opening time in my life so far. Parts of the book were written in my tiny apartment in Burundi, in Kigali Rwanda and Mombasa in Kenya. Nevertheless, there are other books and authors that inspired me before and during the process of writing this novel. Let me briefly explain who and why.

Preface

Much of the history of morality in terms of the two biological traits that aided the human race in developing "the visual and social" comes from bestselling author and public speaker Robert Greene's book *Mastery*.

Nickolas Jordan – The Priest

It all started when I read a book about Burundi in Nigel Watts's *Biography of a Small African Country,* as I needed to know more about my own history. This is where I stumbled upon the burning of Kibimba, where I read the personal testimony of one of the survivors *Matthias Ndimurwanko,* who inspired the story of the teacher who survived the ordeal, giving Nick the bad news about his family. The naïve perspective trait Nick realizes he possesses, was inspired by Robert Greene's book, *Mastery*.

Levy Parker – The Lawyer

The philosophy and ideas behind the "*the philosopher's*

stone" was inspired by *Thomas Aquinas* and *George Marvrodes* in their paper *The Attributes of God*. The idea of turning every negatives into positives, was inspired by Curtis Jackson and Robert Greene's intriguing book, *The 50th Law*. The characteristics of Stan in terms of what women desired in the part where Lucy is engulfed in Stan's presence, was inspired by the characteristics of the Rake in Robert Greene's frightening book, *The Art of Seduction*.

Stan Parker – The Artist

The Power of context by Malcom Gladwell in his wonderful book, *The Tipping Point*, Gladwell is very interesting, and easy to read. As an artist myself, it inspired the part where Nick has a eureka moment on how to help Stan succeed in his art career; or when his mother decided to create a dream team.

Sloane Drexler – The Dreamer

As I was reading *The East African Standard* newspaper early one morning, I stumbled up the children's fable of the hen that could not fly. It was so ingeniously written that I could not help but add it to better explain the consequences of laziness.

Marcus Hammond – The Boss

Finally, during the last days of writing, in my endless search of fables and tales of morality, I first got intrigued by a book called *Greed and Good* written by *Sam Pizzigati*. The book elaborates on inequality, and the anecdote for "the traveler" that can be seen where Nick and Marcus have their session.

Lastly, but not least, the object of my affection are

the tales that can be found in *Budda's Tales for Young and Old* written by Todd Anderson, from which I got the story of the *Two ways of beating a drum*.

Without no doubt, Sant Kirpal Singh is my biggest influence and inspiration for the analyses Nick makes at the end of each story on the seven different vices. Kirpal Singh who's only mission was to fill the human heart with compassion, mercy and universal love.

Acknowledgments

I was inspired, as I seem to always be, by my insightful conversations with my very good friend Aristide Horimbere. His way of seeing the world always makes me laugh and think deeply. Thank you, "Hov".

As always, I prevailed upon my friends and family to critique various drafts of the manuscript. Happily they complied, and *Greener on the Other Side* is infinitely better for it. Many thanks to Kinja Nyakabasa for the endless support and blind faith, Andrea Haragazwe for understanding me, Belise Ntasano for letting me know that I don't know everything and Stephane Kigoma for always keeping it as real as possible.

ABOUT THE AUTHOR

LIONEL NTASANO lives in Bujumbura, Burundi. He was born in the same city but was raised in Zambia. He attended university in the USA, Kenya and Switzerland. He almost quit college to be a member of a music band, and wishes he'd actually had the guts to do it. He now understands that the pain of regret hurts much more than the pain of failure.